# Mary-Anne's
# Famine

# Mary-Anne's Famine

## Colette McCormack

ATTIC PRESS
Dublin

First published in Ireland in 1995 by
Attic Press Ltd
29 Upper Mount Street
Dublin 2


ISBN 1 85594 185 6


The moral right of Colette McCormack to be identified as the author of this work has been asserted.


Cover design: Angela Clarke
Typesetting: Jimmy Lundberg Desktop Publishing
Printing: Guersney Press Co. Ltd


Attic Press receives financial assistance from the
Arts Council/An Comhairle Ealaíon, Ireland.

To my husband, Larry and my children,
Coleen, Lorcán, Shona, Ciara, Seán and Aoife – and
Martina, for their help both practical and loving.
Thank you also to my father,
Frank Evers, and to my brothers and sisters.

To my sounding-board Maria,
whose comments were so helpful.

To my extended family for their suggestions.

To Robin and Hugh.

To my editor, Ríona MacNamara,
whose help and encouragement
were of great help to me.

# <u>ACKNOWLEDGEMENTS</u>

My sincere thanks to the following for all their help in the writing of this book: to Seán Andrews, who loaned me schoolbooks of the Famine era from his collection; to Martin Kelly, who provided useful information on the period; to the librarians in Celbridge and Maynooth, who were so helpful to me at all times; to Daniel of the Irish-American Cultural and Historical Society on Fifth Avenue in New York; to my writing group, the Gateway Project; to Lena Boylan; to Terry Hassett Henry, for all her help; to the Hawker McLoughlin in Buncrana, whose detailed description of the Famine cottage was so useful to me; and also the thatcher of Buncrana who taught me to thatch.

# GLOSSARY

*a stóir* - my dear

*alanna* - pet, darling

*bagáiste* - baggage

*baile mór* - big town

*brea* - lovely, grand

*bruitín* - mashed or pulped potatoes

*caibín* - cap

*ceíli* - to meet, chat and socialise at night

*clochán* - village

*clocking hen* - a hen hatching eggs

*comeallyas* - old familiar songs

*'Dean deifir'* - hurry up, make haste

*dilís* - faithful, loyal, true

*duidín* - clay pipe

*'Fan liom'* - wait for me

*feadóg* - tin whistle

*form* - a long wooden seat, without a back, generally used in schools and for seating in homes

*forninst* - near to or beside

*gearrchaile* - young girl

*gorta* - a ghostly figure symbolising hunger

*'Mais é do thoil é'* - please

*'M'anam, is cailín dathúil gléigeal thú, a stóir'* - Upon my soul, it's a beautiful girl you are, my love

*plantain* - a clump of trees

*poirín* - small potato

*reithe cogaidh* - battering ram

*sceal* - story

*seanchaí* - storyteller

*sléan* - instrument for cutting the sods of turf from the turfbank

*sos* - break, rest; *sos beag* - short break

*sugán* - stools with seats woven from dried rushes

*'Táim ag teacht'* - I am coming

*'Táim go bronach'* - I am heartbroken

*tuirne* - spinning wheel

Extracts from the journal of a fourteen-year-old girl who lived in County Galway in the 1840s. The journal was found when an old outhouse was being demolished to make way for a new house on land in the district of Moneen. The land had been recently purchased by a family from the New England states of America who intended to use the new building as a summer house or holiday retreat. The pages were packed inside an oilskin bag similar to that used by sailors to protect precious documents from damp on board ship. There were two separate sections, one in childish unformed writing and in the Irish language, and the other section beginning with the explanation that the writings had been translated from 'the Irish', by Seán Thornton, schoolmaster, Moneen, County Galway.

# Part One:
# IRELAND

# CHAPTER 1

**Moneen, Co. Galway, Ireland.**

**August 1845**

I WANT you to know who I am, where I come from, and how I live in this time, so you will always remember and pray for me.

My name is Mary-Anne Joyce, and I am fourteen years of age. I live here in Galway with my mam and dad and Mamo Cait. I have no brothers or sisters living – they all died when they were babies. My mam's name is Honor, and my father is Jamesy, and Mamo Cait lives with us.

Our *bothán* is mud-walled, with a thatch roof, and is down a boreen at the butt of the mountain. In the cabin there is a kitchen, then one small room and a loft. There is one window in the kitchen and one in the small room. There are flagstones on the kitchen floor, put down by Dado Mikey before I was born.

Mam and Dad sleep in the small room, and Mamo Cait and me sleep in the settle bed in the kitchen, which is always warm and smoky from the turf fire. The fire never goes dead. At night-time we put pratie skins and ashes over it, and we rake it out in the morning. Mamo blows on the warm embers until they flame, then she puts on the dry sods one by one until they come alight. The fireplace is big and wide with a nook on either side where you can sit. You can see the sky sometimes from the nook when the fire is low and not giving off too much smoke. There is a stone arch over the fire and we hang the rosaries there after the prayers are said at night. The stirabout pot and the kettle hang from the crane over the fire. The griddle and the pot oven are in the nook on one side of the hearth, and the 'pig's pot' is on the other side. The turf for the fire comes from the bog over at Cloncrane. Dad *sléans* the turf out of the bog, and Mam and me catch the wet clods and lay them out to dry. After a few days, if the weather is good, we foot them; then, after more days, we load them on to the creels of the donkey, bring them home and clamp the sods at the gable end.

My dad is a sailor and went away to many countries. He came back to live in Moneen after Dado Mikey died. Dado had stood on a rusty nail and his foot went all black. He was very sick. Mamo put hot cloths and herbs on his foot but it did not get better. We buried him in the field by the chapel at Christmas time two years ago. It is lonesome the place is without him.

Dad made many pieces of furniture for the cabin. He fashioned the forms for along the wall, the *sugán* chairs for beside the fire, and a dresser to put the ware on. He put the thatch on the cabin and the sheds with the straw from the threshings. He gets the lime from the kiln to whitewash the walls inside and out.

When it comes near thrashing time, he fashions the flails from the cuttings of the hazel tree. He covers them with wet eelskins and trades them to the farmers, when harvesting time comes, for meal and straw. He sows the praties, cabbage and turnips in the outside field. We always eat praties at dinner time.

## September 1845

MAM and Dad and me work hard in the fields as there has to be rent money for the man in the Big House. There are a lot of rocks and stones in our fields. We gather them to clear the ground and make walls for around the little fields so the animals do not stray away to the hills. We have a donkey, a cow, a few sheep and the hens. Mam sells the eggs in the *baile mór* on the market day. She will buy homespun to fashion breeches and skirts in the market too. Mamo makes knitting thread from the wool of the sheep with *an tuirne* and she knits ganseys, socks, and wool *caibíns* for the cold days. We have big black shawls to keep us warm out of doors in the winter.

I want to let you know about the praties and the trouble that is on us ... Today when I went to the field I could smell the badness that is on them. There has been a lot of rain and sultry weather which Mamo says is bad and carries the sickness to the crop. We pray the rosary that God and his Blessed Mother will take away the badness and that the praties will come good next year. Mamo tells me of the other times when the praties went bad in other years and people died from hunger. It makes me sad in my heart to think of those times. What will we do if the hunger comes again to Moneen? Mamo says that in those bad days she boiled nettles to eat, and that nettles are good for the blood. The people also collected watercress from the streams and some fish from the lake and rivers. She said she would eat anything when she was very hungry. A lot of people died in those famines. We know that the disease that kills the praties did not damage them on the islands of Aran. Sometimes I think that I would go to the islands if I could. There is a story that the *gorta* has been seen about Moneen. It comes at famine time and moves along the paths at night. I am afraid that I will see it. It looks like a skeleton with light all around it.

My fingers get all sore after all the writing and I put away the pages for another time.

I HELP Mamo to make the rush candles for winter. We get the rushes in the streams and river, and keep them by the fire to dry them, then we dip the pith into goose grease and store them away. Rushes are used for many things. We strew them on the flags in the cold weather, Mam and Mamo weave baskets and creels from them, and Dad weaves the *sugán* seats also. We trade the creels and baskets at the market in the *baile mór*. We must have the money for the rent days. The meal for the bread comes from the threshing. Mam grinds it down and makes corn-meal bread with buttermilk from the churning. The bread is put into the pot oven over hot coals from the fire, and more hot embers are put on the lid, and the bread is cooked through that way. When the bread is ready, Mamo puts it at the window to cool. The butter is made on a Friday with the cream skimmed from the milk crocks. Mam puts the cream into a tin can, puts a piece of muslin on top and then puts on the lid tight. She bangs the can up and down on a pad on her knee until the milk turns. She gathers and shapes the butter with the wooden pats and puts it on a slab in the dairy. We use the buttermilk to make the bread and to drink. I like all the little bits of but-ter that floats on the top and it takes away the thirst.

I like the cowshed at milking time, there is a nice warm smell in it. Mam sits on the three-legged stool and rests her head against the cow's warm belly. She always talks away to the cow as she squeezes the spins and the milk swishes into the bucket. Bid, our cow, chews the cud and flicks her tail at the flies. Sometimes she will give a lash of her tail to your head if the flies were bothering her a lot, but mostly she is gentle and quiet. The other day Mam said to me that it was time I learned how to milk – 'It'd be a great help,' she said. She showed me how to keep the bucket steady between my knees, and how to hold the spins in my two hands, squeezing them until the milk comes out and into the bucket. It was not that easy, the spins were so slippy and Bid kept moving her feet and the milk did not all the time go into the bucket. Mam said not to worry, and that when Bid got to know my hands every-thing would be fine.

In the summer after the milking Bid goes out into the pasture and in the winter she is kept in the shed in the haggard. Our wee donkey is tethered in the small field and the rope is long enough so she can travel a fair distance for grass. Her hooves were all turned up when she came to us first, so Dad pared them down and now they are fine. Sometimes I ride around the field on her back, and she likes to be scratched behind her ears. The hens are very busy creatures, always clucking away and pecking on the grass and greens. I get the eggs in the shed, though some of the hens lay out and I have to go searching the ditches for the nests. Mam puts settings of eggs under the clocking hen, and I love when the little yellow chicks break their way out of the shells. They are sold in the market when they are a few days old.

---

## February 1846

I GO to school across the mountain with Katie Mongan, Mairtín Connor, Bairbre Lidon and Seán Óg McDonagh. Our school is mud-walled with a thatch roof. It was built by the people in time gone by. There is one big room with an earth floor and forms along the walls, and out in the yard is a lavatory shed. Master Thornton teaches reading, writing, arithmetic and the fiddle. We pay a little money to the Master to buy slates, and chalk and books. Master Thornton comes from County Clare, but got the teaching in Dublin and came to live in Clonmore a while ago. We give him the writings to put away in a safe place. He tells us to write all these things down for our children and their children who we will never know. Every day we bring sods of turf to school for the fire and the Master will gather us around the heat and tell stories of the old days. He makes us laugh sometimes. He is a kind man and says not to worry about the potato trouble, that God is good and there is always America where so many of our people have gone before.

In our village we have many neighbours. They come to *ceilí* in our cabin at times and Mamo Cait will play the squeezebox and we do jigs and reels and sets and sing the comeallyas. The hobnails strike sparks off the flagstones in the dancing. The *seanchaí* tells tales of other times and places and people until near the sunrise. Mam, Dad, Mamo and me go to *ceilí* in other kitchens other times. Mamo Cait smokes her *duidín* and rambles on about when she was young. She got her schooling in the hedge school because the law said that no children were to have the learning. The schoolmaster would have the classes behind the hedges and in the *plantains* and if he was caught he would be put in jail. So that no one of the law would know that there had been lessons in a place, the boys and girls would bring a sod of turf to sit on during the class and when it was finished they would bring the sod of turf home again with them. There would be no sign left that there had been a school class in that place that day.

Mamo tells that the priests were stopped from saying the Mass, and that there were Mass rocks in many places, and a Mass path on which people would go to Mass out of sight of the law. She told about the 'Ark of Kilbaha' in County Clare, which was like an altar made to be carried by four men to the strand when the tide was out, and the priest could say Mass there in safety. The 'Ark' was made of wood and had four carrying handles. Master Thornton says that he saw it when he lived in his home in County Clare.

## March 1846

WE take the Mass path to our chapel which is at the back of the hill. The chapel is very old and is mud-walled like the cabins around it. We stand on the earth floor during the Mass. The name of our chapel is St Kevin's. The priest is Father O'Rourke. He comes in his horse and cart to say the Mass. He says that we must pray that the disease on the praties will not linger. He says that if things do not get better we should be thinking of taking the boat to America; it is better to leave than to die from the hunger. I would not like to go away from Moneen forever. I would never see Katie or Mairtín or any of my friends again. America is a big country and a long way off. There is work and plenty of money over there and no famine, but it isn't Moneen. Mam says that Father O'Rourke has helped people to travel there many a time, she says that he would give you the coat off his back if you needed it. I do not want the coat off his back. I do not want to go away.

## March 1846, St Patrick's Day.

THIS is the day to put in the seed praties. Dad has not many good seed praties this year. Some of them are black and soft and smell bad. We help with the dropping of the good seed in the 'lazy beds' which lie in the shelter of the walls. As the earth is not so good and is scarce, we put kelp on the ground to build up the beds. Mam and me carry the kelp up from the sea shore in the turf creels, and pile it at the wall. There is so much rock in the ground that there is not much space for tilling. Sometimes Dad will lever big rocks up out of the ground and every little bit of the earth under it is welcome. You have to scratch a living out of the ground, so my father says. In the summer time lovely heathers and wild flowers grow between the rocks, and the colours of the rocks seem to change with the colour of the flowers and wee plants and no longer are they grey and dismal. I like to climb the hill some days and look down over the *clocháns*. It is a lovely spot when the sun is shining, the plants are thriving and the flowers are showing amid the rocks. I can see the smoke rising and the people and the animals in the fields. I come up here to do the writings for the Master. Yesterday I asked him what more there is to put down. He says, 'Write what you see, how you think, about what happens in the village, your family. Our times are hard times, *gearrchaile*, and in time to come our people should know of these things.'

# April 1846

THE green leaves are just showing in the 'lazy beds'. We watch them every day. The distemper has not come, though the rain is very heavy. I hear that in some places people cover the new shoots with cloths to try to keep the badness from falling from the sky on to them, but Dad says he fears the disease is already in the ground, and that the rain and sultry weather help it grow and rot the new potatoes. The neighbours take turns to watch over the new green leaves. They lean over the walls and stay for many an hour. Me and Katie stay for a time too when school is over.

At Mass on Sunday Father O'Rourke had a message from the Government telling the people how to get some good out of the bad praties. They should be mashed into a dish and the *bruitín* should be washed and dried on the griddle. Oatmeal or flour should be mashed in to the *bruitín* along with the starch from the washing of the praties, formed into a cake and eaten. Nobody thinks much of this idea, but Father O'Rourke says that we must make an effort, and that we are to support and help each other in this time of trouble.

# May 1846

## This is my birthday month -
## Our Lady's month.

KATIE, Mairtín, Seán Óg and me had a happy time this day on the way home from school. Seán Óg made a ball of twists of hay and old rags and we made hurley sticks from the *aiteann* bush. We played in the fields and along the boreens all the way home. We go without our boots these warm days and the dust rises around our bare feet and in between our toes. We walk in the mountain streams to cool and to clean the dust away, and we splash the water on each other. When the thirst comes on us the clear brown water in the streams is cold and lovely to drink.

Master Thornton gave me great praise today about the way I am writing down all the happenings around Moneen. I tell him that sometimes my hand gets weary from it, and he says to take a *sos beag* and go back to it on another day.

Mam says that, thank God, there does not appear to be anything wrong with the praties so far, the green leaves are growing tall and strong in their beds. And Mamo says that maybe the bad times are behind us. Our potato pit is as good as empty, though. Mam counts the praties into the pot these days, though there was a time when they were plentiful that she'd fill the pot to the brim, and when they were cooked she would empty them out on to a big platter on the middle of the table. She boils cabbage as well to go along with the few praties. I gather the nettles to be cooked too. We eat them though they have a strange taste. Mamo makes us drink the nettle water, she says there is a lot of good in it. There are some of the roots that I do not like and I 'turn up my nose', as Mam says, but she tells that some day I'll chase a crow for the likes of these. My father says that we will struggle on until the new crop comes in. There are many worse off than we are, we hear stories of workhouses, of disease and of many people dying from the hunger. There is a great dread in me when I hear these tales, and big and all as I am I shelter my head on Mam's knee and she says, 'Wheest, *alanna*, don't be fretting yourself, we'll get by.'

In school these days there are not so many children. Master Thornton tells us many *sceals* when the lessons are over and we are having a *sos*. We hear about the ship that went aground off the Kerry coast. The ship split in two and many sailors drowned. There was wheat on board, so the people rowed out and took ashore the wheat and many people lived because of this food. He told us about the Big Wind of '39 and the havoc it caused. The people used to say this prayer after that happening: 'May the fort we are in be a solid castle, the enemies pursuing us be blind, the Holy Ghost amongst us, may He put His shield above us.' We hear of the priest, Father Mathew, who tells the people to give up drinking the 'odious whiskey' and to take the Temperance Medal.

## June 1846

THE weather is so very warm and there is a lot of rain; the Master says we are having a heatwave. We wear our heavy boots no more in this weather, bare feet tracking through the squelchy fields. Now that it is warm the hunger is not so bad. We eat greens and bread made from the grain the Government sends, and Dad sets snares for the rabbits. He and the neighbours set them at night so the man in the Big House does not find out. The bread has a terrible taste and is very hard to chew, but it will keep us going.

Our praties are still green, thanks be to God and His Holy Mother.

GOD help us all. It is here, it is on the praties ... The blackness is on our new praties. Peter O'Malley banged on the doors in the early hours shouting for us to come out. Mamo went in her shift, no boots – Dad and Mam too. All the neighbours came out of their cabins moaning and crying. Peter said he had seen a thick white mist up on the mountain when he was coming over yesterday and now all the grand green growths are covered with disease. The leaves are all brown and black and they hang down and the bad smell is back again lying over the fields. The people were shouting and crying and swearing – no one could believe what they were seeing. I saw the fear in the faces and I couldn't stop shivering. Mam and Dad had tears running down their faces and were holding each other. I put my two arms around them and Mamo came and put her arms around us all.

We went back in home. Dad said to close the door, for we do not want people to see us in this sad time. Mamo went to her corner and sat in her chair with her apron over her head, keening, and saying over and over, 'What's to become of us? What's to become of us?' Mam and Dad just stood there, not saying anything.

After a time Dad said to Mamo to hould her wheest and to get herself together, and that we'd go out and dig up the pratie stalks and see what could be got from them.

The neighbours came in twos and threes and we all started to dig. The disease had got to some of the *poiríns* already, and we scrabbled in the clay to find any good ones there was. We filled a couple of baskets with the *poiríns* and we made a fresh pit for them. Dad says that we'd maybe get a month out of them with care, and they are what we would have put in the pig's pot.


## August 1846

I DO not find it easy to write for Master Thornton, the very bad way things are with us these days. There is not much to eat, for we have used up what was stored away. All our hens are gone, so we have no eggs to eat or sell. We sold our sheep for very little, and our cow and our wee donkey. We scour the pratie patches to find even one good one, and Dad says there is no seed for next year.

The man from the Big House gave us some money, but he says that after it is gone we will have to forage for ourselves, as he is in hard times too. But there is not one thing left to buy with the money – no grain, no vegetables. When Dad goes to the *baile mór* he comes back with the makings of a small cake, nothing more. The soup kitchens are near us and we must make use of them. Father

O'Rourke tells us never to mind that the people who give out the soup are not of our religion, to live is the important thing. Some people turn from being Catholics so they will get more soup and other help. We drink the soup but it is not very good. Mamo's poor legs are giving her trouble. Dad carries her on his back at times.

There are people called the Friends who have come to our parish to help us in our trouble and hunger. Many of our neighbours in the other villages are out of their houses because there was no money for the landlords. The law came and smashed the doors in with the *reithe cogaidh* and broke the windows and thrun all the beds and chairs out in the yard. Some of the poor people went to the workhouse in Galway, and some of them made shelters in the hedges and ditches. There is so much crying and moaning about the place.

A LETTER from America today. Ten dollars from Uncle Arthur and Aunt Bina. The letter said that if we want to come to America, Arthur will send us more, and we are to learn the English for if we haven't got it, it's no use us thinking of looking for work in the big cities. Dad says we will have to keep in mind that we might be driven to going away whether we like it or not. The ten dollars is a mighty lot of money and should buy meal for a while more, and with any scrapings we can find in the fields and ditches we will struggle on ... God bless Uncle Arthur and Aunt Bina, they are so good to think of us. Mamo says that they are the answer to her prayers. Her poor legs are very bad now.

## December 1846

MAMO Cait died a week last Saturday. She got the famine fever and the black leg and there was nothing the doctor could do for her. He is a sick man himself. He sent her to the fever sheds but she did not come home to us again. Master Thornton came with his horse and cart to bring her to the chapel. There are no coffins left. We buried her beside Dado Mikey. There is so much sadness all round Moneen.

## January 1847

WE are going away to America. There is no place for us now in Ireland. Dad says that we will go while the going is good and while we have strength in our legs. Father O'Rourke is finding out about the fares and the boat, and seeing who wants to come with him from around the parish. He will stay out in the United States with us until we are all settled. Master Thornton is teaching us English. Uncle Arthur sent another letter and he said to us that he will look after us when we arrive there. The boat that we will be going on will be travelling in my birthday month, May.

## March 1847

THERE is a great hunger on all of us. Only the soup is keeping us from falling down. The meal is scarce. A lot of people have died in Moneen.

## April 1847

TODAY I walk up to the hill and look down on the village. There is no smoke rising, no sign of life. The fields are empty – there are no sheep or cattle, no hens, – the land is bare of everything. The green is coming between the rocks, and the wee flowers won't see me this year. Will flowers grow in the places we are going to? My hunger pains and my sadness pains are all mixed up in me. We are going away from Moneen. Will I ever see this spot again?

I will give these last pages to Master Thornton tomorrow. He will help us to bring our few things to the boat in Galway. He is not going away yet, he says. Maybe he will go to another part of Ireland, but not to America – not yet.

# CHAPTER 2

SEÁN Thornton studied the grubby, tear-stained pages. Poor Mary-Anne – these were the last pages of the 'writings', as she was wont to call the work of describing life in and around Moneen which had been set as a task by himself in school. The Joyce family was one of the families, organised by Father O'Rourke, from the parish who would be travelling to the New World of America in search of a new life for themselves. He knew that the *Clarence* was the boat which would be picking up the group and sailing out from Galway in May, as Jamesy Joyce had asked him for the use of his horse and cart to bring their few meagre belongings to the docks. It would be the last job Seán would do around the area. He had helped in the transporting of the dead to the graveyards, a harrowing experience each time. Since coffins were no longer available, the dead had to be buried in the clothes they died in. Seán felt the weight of his twenty-three years pressing heavily on him. The anguish and despair all around him was fearsome. He could not stay much longer in this hellhole which was Connacht.

Next week the Joyce family would close the door of their cabin behind them for the last time. A hardworking, industrious family, they had been independent in so far as they could. Now they could no longer continue. Death was the only certainty facing them in Moneen. They were taking a great chance in going, but they would be taking a greater one if they remained. Seán wondered how the people would survive the months of travel ahead of them. Granted, Father O'Rourke was accompanying the group and would stay with them until they were settled. Rumour had it, though, that the months on board ship in primitive conditions caused many premature deaths and rendered those who survived unable for the rough-and-tumble of competition for work in the land across the Atlantic. Seán decided that he would suggest to Mary-Anne that she might write to him about life on the boat and her experiences once she had arrived in America. He realised that she was a remarkably perceptive girl, old beyond her years. He felt in his bones that it was vital that this information should be passed on to future generations, and he would try to impress on Mary-Anne the importance of continuing with her journal as best she could.

TWO months later Seán Thornton reached the city of Dublin. Footsore, heartsore and weary, he looked at the teeming streets and could not believe the opulence around him. Well-dressed ladies and fashionable men strolled the elegant thoroughfares, and horse-drawn carriages with stately coachmen in splendid uniforms clattered by, their precious cargoes protected behind curtains from the dusty street.

He had passed through the most horrific sights on his long journey to the capital city. He had seen workhouses whose windows were filled with wild-eyed starving men, women and children, their hands held out in supplication. Bodies lay along the rough roads for weeks without burial. The smells were overwhelming, the horror unbelievable, and yet, here in Dublin there was no sign of distress, starvation or other horrors. No troubled people here. It was as if there were two different Irelands, two different worlds. How could this be? He recalled reading about Daniel O'Connell, the Liberator, dead these three months. O'Connell had died a broken man, a man who had seen his life's work come to naught. In the previous February he had taken part in the debate about the Soup Kitchens Act, but he had been in such poor health that his last words, spoken in low tones, had been heard by just a few. 'Ireland is in your hands, in your power. If you do not save her she cannot save herself...'

Seán thought, looking around him, that in Dublin at least there was no obvious sign of need for 'saving' or 'rescuing'. He felt bitter and angry, remembering the desperation and agony of the poor of the West and those on the roads to Dublin.

The weather during his journey had been simply superb: blue skies, soft breezes, the countryside looking its best. At odds, indeed with what he had seen on his travels to the east coast: dead bodies, half-naked wandering people, the hovels, some smashed down by the infamous battering-ram, the makeshift hedge and ditch homes, inhabited by gaunt, yellow-faced, despair-ridden people. He felt a growing resentment as he stood on Sackville Street and observed the carefree comings and goings of the people. To all outward appearances they were untouched by the agony of rural Ireland.

He roused himself and set about finding the headquarters of the Society of Friends. Over the past couple of years, his contact with those good people in Galway had been inspiring. He planned to seek employment as a schoolteacher through their good offices. He had to do something with his life, get some sense of order into it, otherwise he would drown in the misery surrounding him. His school in Moneen was no longer viable: no children, the entire village in ruins. Clonmore was in the same sad condition, the people driven from their homes by hunger and deprivation. There were many closed cabin doors in the West of Ireland, their owners gone to America. The lucky ones, that is – others lay uncoffined in the parish graveyards, while still more roamed the lanes and boreens, half-demented by the calamities showered on them ...

Clothed, bathed and refreshed, Seán started out on the road for the long trek to Ballycromane, where he had been informed by the Director of the Society of Friends that there was a school which required a schoolmaster. This school was being set up for the education of the poor children of the area by the benevolent wife of a wealthy landlord, who farmed many hundreds of acres in County Wexford. The Honourable Anne Salford-Broone was in need of an experienced male teacher to take charge of a thirty-two-pupil school, which had both boys and girls on its roll. She had provided a two-roomed cottage on her estate for use as a school, and would pay the teacher partly from her own pocket and partly from a fund set up among her peers for the provision of such a school. The Director had spoken with some reticence of this lady, and of her autocratic attitude to those around her. 'Lady Bountiful' was the term used in a kindly way by his friend in the Society, who gave fair warning to Seán that if he succeeded in the interview and if he did pass and obtain the position at the school, he was to tread very carefully, as there was a slight difference of opinion between the local parish priest and the lady who had set up the school. Seán was well aware of the divisions in the school system in the country, and was no way desirous of getting involved in any conflict there might be awaiting him in Ballycromane.

He had some money in his pockets, warm clothing, and a pair of stout boots, all provided by the good people in the Society. He boarded the train for the long trip to the county of Wexford and his new life. The train chugged its steamy way through lovely countryside, lush meadows and golden cornfields, past the outskirts of towns and villages. It was comfortable enough, so he sat back and read again the letter from Mary-Anne written on board the *Clarence*.

# Part Two:
# IRELAND
# &
# AMERICA

# CHAPTER 3

**Letter from Mary-Anne Joyce to
Seán Thornton.**

**May 1847 to June 1847**

Dear Master Thornton,

IT WAS very lonely for us when you said goodbye and
we watched you go away, it near broke our hearts. The
wailing and sobbing of those going away and those
staying behind was something terrible. It must be like
dying. There were people there who would never see their
families again and they were holding and kissing them for
the last time. I know that I will never be able to stay away
forever from Ireland and Moneen. This 'great' new world
we are going to will never be home to me.

After you went away, we lined up for 'rollcall' and a
medical check before we went below deck to where we
are to live and sleep and eat for the length of the travelling
to America. Father O'Rourke had the papers all sorted and
ready for inspection by the officers of the ship, and then
we went below with all our bits and pieces.

Dad and Mam and me share a bunk in the steerage
section. There is not much space for us and our *bagáiste*,
but we are lucky as we have more space than most, as the
bunk space is supposed to be for four people. The
O'Flahertys and the Maughans are near enough to us
so we can talk together and, as Mam says, 'console
ourselves'.

There is no place for 'sanitation', and a lot of people
complain about this. There are chamber pots like at home,

but there is no place private to use them. There are what are called 'closets' on the top decks, but after the few days we are here they are awful dirty and the smell is wicked. It is very hard to sleep at night with the ship going from side to side and up and down, and with the heat. Most of us have been very seasick, and the crying of the babies and little children and the moaning of the people makes me cover my ears and press hard on them to keep me from hearing all the noises.

There is a bad smell below deck. It makes your eyes watery and your throat sore. There is not much air down here. We get to walk up on the top deck for ten minutes in the morning and in the evening if the weather is good. I do look up at the sky and see the sun and wonder if it is shining over Moneen, and when the stars are high in the sky I feel so far away from home.

What are the people doing in the village? Are they starving, roaming the boreens and fields, searching for food as we did before we took the boat? I think of you and school and Mamo and Dado and Mairtín and Katie and all my friends who are buried in the church field, and I can't stop from crying.

WE are twenty days on the boat today, twenty days away from Ireland. A wee baby died two days ago, it made us all very sad. The weather is better today, and we can go up on deck for longer, but there is nothing to see but green water. It is terrible hard to have to go down below after the fresh air. Sometimes, Master Seán, when the ship's men are giving out the rations, the people do push and shove, and oftentimes someone will fall down and do be near walked over. Dad says we are blessed that the Captain is a good honest man and that the rations are never short. The space to cook in is small but we do the best we can. There is a lot of whiskey to be got for the buying, but I am not so happy when there are a lot of people drunk and roaring and shouting, and making another bad smell to go with the other smells there already.

When I am sick and feel so bad and the waves are high, near to the top sail, I think that maybe I will die and leave this awful place. Then I remember Moneen and the fields and the rivers and the mountains, and I keep these thoughts in my head and close my mind to the bad things in this dark and dismal place. Father O'Rourke says we will all feel better soon, that the sickness will pass and we will all sing and dance again. I do not know if he is right about that.

It is hard to know when it is night or day, the weather had turned bad again and no one can go up on deck. People are fighting and complaining. There is not enough water. Last night there was a big fight between two men, and the women were screaming and crying. Father O'Rourke gathered us together forninst the gangway and told us about the great country we are going to, and promised us that all this trouble would soon be over, and we will never be hungry or thirsty again.

MASTER Thornton – today we are thirty days at sea. Mam is so very sick and can hardly sit up. The ship's doctor came and looked at her, he said she might have 'ship fever'. Dad and me sit by her all the time. Her face and hands are so hot, and we put cloths dipped in a little of the drinking water on her poor head to cool her a bit. She says, 'I'm all right, don't be fretting now, it won't be long more.'

The days are going so slowly. Sometimes at night I do dream that we are all at home and we are all as we were before the bad praties. When I wake and know where I am I do think that I will just lay down and die.

Mam is not getting any worse, thanks be to God. I am good at the bit of cooking now and Dad says I am good enough to earn my living at it. He makes me laugh when he says this, but he is only joking me. We cook on a strange sort of fire. It is like a big wooden case, lined with bricks, and the coals are kept in with bars across the front. When everyone has finished their bit of cooking a sailor comes and douses the cooking coals with water because of the danger of a fire catching hold. The food is not always cooked through, as so many want to take their turn, but we get by all right, although there is a great amount of steam about the place at cooking time.

The captain of the boat came below deck today to say that in a few more days we will see sight of the land. People clapped and cheered and some got up and danced around the place. Father O'Rourke gathered us all together and we said the Rosary in thanks for a safe journey.

We are so tired and weary of the shifting ground under our feet. The rations are getting short, but, thank God, no one else has died on the journey save the wee baby. The captain asked if anyone had letters to go back to Ireland when the ship makes the return journey. I will finish this to you when we are settled.


TODAY, forty days after leaving Galway, we see the outline of land, America, our new home.

I cannot say how I feel just now. Everyone is glad that the long journey is almost over. I think that everyone has forgotten the people at home. This makes me very contrary, and I want to sit down on the ground and say, 'No, no, I do not want to be here in this new land, I want to go home.' I want to scream and shout, and I feel frightened that I will never see my village and my friends ever again, and I can't bear the sadness ...

Mam and Dad send their good wishes to you, and we all hope that you will keep well.

From Mary-Anne Joyce.

# CHAPTER 4

SEÁN tucked the letter back into his bag and, resting his head against the cool window, thought about how one's life could be completely changed in a matter of weeks. Mary-Anne's description of life aboard the ship taking her and her family to America had disturbed him; she had hardly skimmed the surface in her descriptions of the miserable journey, he considered, but the heartbreak in the simple sentences was obvious.

He had written a short letter to the Joyce family and handed it in to the shipping authorities in Galway for delivery to them when the *Clarence* made a return journey to the States. In this letter he had told them of his decision to leave Moneen and go to the east coast and try to find some work. He asked that they not forget him and that Mary-Anne should continue to put down in writing her impressions of life in that great country, and he remained their friend Seán Thornton.

He wished to maintain contact with the Joyce family, and as he thought about them he felt a wave of loneliness wash over him. His home and family gone, a stranger in this part of Ireland, no familiar stone walls, no lakes, no mountains... Perhaps he should have left with the rest; surely emigration with those near and dear to you was preferable to working and living with those so different to the warm friendly people of Galway. He was still only twenty-three, but he felt so much more just now. He wished he could roll back the years to the old days when life was easy and happy.

The train pulled into the station at Clonavoe. He descended and rested his travelling bag on the low stone wall as he waited to be taken to Cromane House, the home of the Salford-Broones, and his new life ...

# Letter from Seán Thornton to Mary-Anne Joyce.

## September 1847

MARY-ANNE, I have begun my teaching life again far away from Moneen and Galway. I am in charge of a school with thirty-two pupils, eighteen boys and fourteen girls. The school has two rooms, one for the infants, of whom there are twenty, and the bigger boys and girls are in the other room. There is another teacher, Miss Phoebe Chapman, a timid girl, but a good teacher of the infants. She also teaches sewing to the older girls.

Lady Anne Salford-Broone is the person who has set up this school for 'the education of poor children'. She is a tall, stout lady, with a high colour and strong ideas.

At the end of my train journey from Dublin I was met at the station by one of the men employed at the estate with a pony and trap to convey me the remainder of the journey to Cromane House, a distance of about five miles. The house is a fine handsome building set amidst great gardens, so different from what we know. There are four children in the family, three boys and one girl. The boys are at boarding school in England, and the daughter, Miss Jane, has a governess. My quarters, as I will be 'living in', are on the third floor: two rooms and a convenience, plain and comfortable. I eat all my meals in the kitchen below stairs with the house staff. There are four people employed indoors, while outside there is a gardener for the house gardens and several labouring men to work the land. Miss Marguerite Pym, a rather stern-looking lady, runs the household under the direction of Lady Anne. The Master allows land to his tenants and collects rents from them, the same as in Moneen. Since I have come here I have walked all around and have seen that people working their piece of ground seem to be managing to survive, and so far there are no signs of the stark hunger I have witnessed in the West.

I feel that I will enjoy my work in this part of the country. The school is well kept, and the children appear bright and eager to learn.

To other things. Mary-Anne, how are you and your family? Is life treating you well? I wish only the very best for you and all the people who have had to go away to survive. The hunger is still here, in some places worse than others; the east coast has managed to carry on, as the people here are not so dependent on the potato. There are fevers and diseases about now that haven't been heard of before. The newspapers give the news from the really badly affected areas of the country.

There is a lot of unrest throughout Ireland because of the way the Government is dealing with the Famine. There is a Lord Trevelyan, a hard and unjust man to my way of thinking. He lives a very comfortable life himself, but begrudges the soup kitchens to the poor. Mary-Anne, I say to you that the poor and oppressed will rise against this treatment. Do you know that food is being shipped out of this country every day? Every day of the week sheep, cows, lambs, pigs, wheat, barley flour – all this food – goes to feed other people in other countries. It is very hard to lay blame on those who attack these shipments and the men who help to export this food away from a dying nation. The law should understand the actions of desperate people and be lenient in its sentencing, but not so, I fear.

## October 1847

MARY-ANNE, I have not had much opportunity up to now to continue with this letter to you, but now that the nights are drawing in, it gives me more time to write and let you know how life is over here.

School is going very well. I find that the children are of good behaviour, and anxious to learn. Miss Chapman is a conscientious lady and we work together without rancour. She teaches sewing and knitting to the older girls, and hers is a very industrious group. She lodges in the village convenient to the school.

Lady Anne visits the school on occasions and listens to the children's work; some of them are now on the second book, and one or two of the brighter ones have even reached the third book. Today she came to call and we did some work from the fifth lesson in the *Second Book of Lessons*, all about The Horse.

*'How fast the horse trots! A small boy sits on his back, and holds the reins. The horse is so strong that he could throw off the boy, if he chose, and go his own way. But he is good and tame, and he goes where the boy wants him to go. The boy is kind to his horse, and does not beat him, but pats him on the neck, and speaks to him. Some boys will beat a poor horse and use it ill; I hope you will not be like them.'*

These are the simple lessons we are now learning, and the children love to get their chance to stand up and read for her ladyship. Do you remember the lessons from the second book? Remember your favourite lesson? It was Lesson 22, on 'Plants, Flowers, and Seeds'. I recall very well indeed how you loved to recite 'We Must Not Be Idle', the poem at the end of the lesson 'How doth the little busy bee improve each shining hour'.

Happy memories, Mary-Anne.

# November 1847

MANY more days and weeks have passed by and I have not completed this letter. Times are not improving. Lately, I have noticed a lassitude among some of the younger children, and a tendency to fall asleep during lessons. I fear this is not caused by indifference to their lessons, but by something more worrying. Miss Pym, the housekeeper at the House, gives me left-overs from the weekly dinner-parties there to distribute to the children. I have noticed they will take home this precious food, uneaten, to share with the less fortunate families.

**Some weeks later.**

TIMES are coming bad, Mary-Anne. My poor children are getting pinched-looking, their eyes larger and their faces pale. Any surfeit of food there was comes not so often now. There is 'cheese paring' going on at the House, Miss Pym tells me, so food parcels for the children are few and far between. It is of great help to me to be able to tell you of these things; to share my worries and fears with someone is a great solace.

It will be Christmas time before you receive my letter.

Two visitors to the school today. Lady Anne, full of her problems, the cost of living, the fees for her sons in school in England, the diseases and plagues sweeping through the country, the little money to be made in farming – indeed she was much agitated when taking her leave of us. I consider that she did not truly observe the children.

Father O'Beirne was next. A gentle kindly soul, he is deeply upset at the happenings. 'What did we do to deserve this?' he asked me. 'All the poor people are in terrible want.' He asked me to accompany him on his visits after school. 'I need an extra pair of shoulders to give me the courage to keep going,' he said. I agreed to go with him.

My heart is indeed heavy, Mary-Anne. Some of the sights we saw on our visits would only deepen your despair. Dark, dank cabins, the people within with no spirit left to move them, little children, white-faced and weak; some of them refusing soup for fear of God knows what. The priest urged them to drink up and have sense. Some of the cottages are neat and clean, but the dungheaps, the air of poverty and despair, are prevailing everywhere. Are we a lazy indolent race? I begin to question. Or is our spirit forever broken? I can write no more this day ...

## December 1847

THE lady of the house came to school today to tell the children how to make a nourishing meal from herbs and roots... My pale, thin little children looked at her incomprehendingly. Poor foolish woman – does she not realise that she is dealing with small beings who have lost the power to think, let alone listen and take note of a cooking recipe? Has she ever experienced the pains of hunger, ever known the terror of not knowing from one day to the next if food can be found? She has a good heart, but no imagination.

## January 1848

YOU are probably thinking that you will never hear from me again. The New Year, what will it bring us? This letter is full of discontent and woe – you will not be wanting to read much more of it.

I try to distribute gleanings from the kitchens in the House to my poor hungry little children; they will come in their rags for a little. Lady Anne has declared her intention of sewing some 'shifts' for the 'poor creatures', and will enlist the help of her friends. It is hard for her to realise that clothes are not an absolute necessity for the hungry.

Today the Inspector of Schools came to visit us, accompanied by Lady A. He remarked that he was pleased at the bright, clean classroom, the well-dressed children. The new 'shifts' made their appearance a day or so ago. He must have observed the large-eyed pale faces before him with some dismay, but forbore to say anything until he was leaving, when he said to me, as he placed five shillings in my hand, 'Do what you can with this, it is a very sad time for us.'

Lady Anne was bursting with pride at the praise of 'her' school, and spoke to Miss Chapman and myself, before she took her leave, of her pleasure at the good work we were doing, and of her pride in her 'little school'.

God bless you, Mary-Anne.

Your friend, Seán Thornton.


## Letter from Mary-Anne Joyce to Seán Thornton

### July - August 1847

Dear Master Thornton,

A FURTHER letter to tell you how we are doing over here. When we stepped from the boat onto the land I felt my head go round and round. So many people, so much noise – the strange smells and languages of America set me astray. I looked away out to the ocean and thought if I opened wide my eyes and looked hard enough across the water, I could almost see Ireland from here. But, alas, only green water before me, as far as could be. The sick people from below deck were carried up the gangways by the strongest of the men. Their faces were yellow, and so thin were their legs that they sank down on the ground and remained there. Father O'Rourke gathered those of us from Moneen and Clonmore together, and with our bits and pieces we went through the gates into a very big room with a ceiling so far over us you could almost not see it. Our papers were looked at and we had to show our tongues to the guards, for why I do not know. People were pushing and moving here and there, and children were crying everywhere. Dad said to hold on to his coattails. When we finished the business with the law we trailed on to the dock, pulling our bundles after us. There was a vast crowd of persons behind the fences. Dad had made a big paper sign with 'James, Honor and Mary-Anne Joyce' on it in black letters, which we held up high to help Uncle Arthur to find us in this very crowded place. Poor Mam was weak and leaned on me.

The loneliness is back on me again. What are we doing here in this strange noisy world?

Mam and me kept our arms tight around each other. Then there was a great shouting and roaring and Uncle Arthur, for it was he, came running. He was crying and saying 'Jamesy, Jamesy, is it you that's in it, and Honor and the child?' He hugged us all and then stood back and said, 'May the good God look down on us all this day.' We were ragged and sick and weary and no flesh much on our bones, and I could tell by his face that he was put out by how we were. We all just stood there and looked at each other, and then Uncle Arthur said, 'We'll go home now.' My heart jumped, thinking that he meant home to Galway, but no. *Táim go brónach...*


## Three weeks later.

MASTER Seán, I am putting down what life is like in New York City.

Uncle Arthur and Aunt Bina live on the lower East Side in a small apartment. Arthur is a farrier and he shoes the horses for the families who have large houses with many rooms upstairs and down. These people live in a place called Gramercy Avenue, and they drive handsome carriages drawn by two horses mostly. Uncle Arthur got Dad a job helping him to make the shoes for these horses and others besides. When Aunt Bina came to this country at my age she worked in one of these fine houses for a rich family. 'Hard work for little money – don't believe those who tell you there is gold on the streets of America,' she said. 'Work your fingers to the bone for many's a long day and night, and no gold at the end of it.' She laughs when she says this, but you can see that she means it.

Where we are now living is crowded with many people from many other countries. Our room is on the second floor of a high house and it is all Irish people who live in this building. The ceilings in the rooms are high and the windows wide, but it is so very warm we cannot sleep at night. Mam and me sometimes sit out on the stoop for a 'breath of fresh air'. It is seldom a breeze comes, but when it does and it touches my face I am so thankful for it. Our clothes cling to us with the damp heat, and the water runs down our faces and arms. You just cannot understand what it is like, this heavy heat.

The children around here play on the streets and they swing on the backs of the hansom cabs as they pass by. The poor horses are steaming hot. Some of them rest next to our building with their nosebags on and Bina always has water ready for them.

Dad and Arthur shoe the horses at the forge, and they are busy night and day. Mam and Bina sew curtains and bedcovers for the stores. I am learning to work with fine threads, and lacework as Mamo used to want me to do. I do collars and sleeve trims for the fine ladies in Gramercy already. Bina says my work is lovely. Poor Mamo, if she knew this she would be pleased.

There is a railing around the grass in the front of these houses, and this is called the park. Only the people who live in the houses there can use the park. The nursemaids take the small children to play there. Bina says that each family living there have a key so they can use it as they wish. Mam and me, if we walk in that direction, often stand at the railings, wishing for a touch of the grass on our poor hot feet.

## August 1847

WHEN the heat of this summer presses down on us, Dad and Mam talk about the summers at home, the cool mountain breezes and the clean, clear brown water running down to the plains.

We are in America now for going on two months. We are eating well, and all our bony parts have been well covered. Mam looks well and has got some new clothes, as has Dad. They work long hours but we are never short of food or water. Dad says he may go to look for some land in the country when he has enough put by.

The weather is still very hot. The families in our side of the building sleep out on the roof at times for the air. There are two families from Clonmore living in our house, the O'Flahertys and the Kellys. They call most Sundays after Mass. They are finding it hard to settle, and talk constantly of going home. Dad says, 'Home to what?' and Mrs O'Flaherty says, 'Home to where I belong.' She sheds tears sometimes and Mr O'Flaherty says, 'For God's sake, woman, have you forgotten the hardship back in Ireland?'

Not all of us who came with Father O'Rourke have got work. He went to the Cathedral to ask the bishops to help and some of the men were lucky. As they are mostly farming men, life in the city is not what they are used to. The women scrub floors in the big houses, and do the laundry. The older girls work in the sewing rooms in the factories, all crowded together with not much air. We have had no word how things be at Moneen – there is no one of the neighbours left to write to us.

There are many people here who hate the Government and the landlords for having to leave their homes and come to this country, in which, though we eat well and get by on what we earn, we will never feel at home. Many long to return to Ireland, as I do. It is a constant thought in my head. I cannot even see the sky for all the high buildings closing it away from me, just a small patch of blue. The heat of the sun burns into everyone and everything, yet I cannot see it over my head like at home.

I got your letter saying you were leaving Moneen and going across the country to Dublin. I hope you are happy and have got a pleasant and comfortable place to live, and that you are not hungry or unhappy.

I held the cover of your letter in my hand, knowing that it had been in your hand and in the air of Ireland. Your letters are a great comfort to us, and please do not stop writing of how things are with you.

I look out for your next letter. I am sending you the 'writings' from this new land as you asked. I am content to know that when you open this letter from me some of my dreams and longings will enter the air around you and a part of me will be home again in Ireland.

Mam and Dad ask to be remembered to you.

Your friend, Mary-Anne.

# Letter from Seán Thornton to Mary-Anne Joyce.

## March 1848

My dear Mary-Anne,

SO many things have occurred since I last took pen to paper to write to you...

There is an organisation here called the 'Young Irelanders', and I am considering becoming a member of it. There is so much badness going on here at the behest of the Government. There is food going out of the country at a great rate to feed the people across the water, and none for the starving Irish. God in his heaven must be giving the 'blind eye' to such carry-on, else he would wreak some destruction on these vile people. There is no one to stand up and say, 'No more, feed our own first', so it seems to me that this a breeding ground for trouble. Are we Irish rated as 'stupid and useless', people who will take all insults and indignities which the people who govern our country, however unjustly, heap on to us? High rents, heavy taxes – they are grinding us into the ground, and for why? We could govern ourselves, given half a chance. There are many more who feel as I do, mark my words. Injustice breeds trouble.

As you know, Mary-Anne, I am a peace-loving man, and I avoid confrontation ... but for how much longer? I look around and see nothing for the people of Ireland but rebellion. We may be hungry and fever-ridden, but there is a spark lying dormant in many which needs only a leader to inspire and rouse us to fend for ourselves and not be dependent on the Sasanach.....

Fighting words from a schoolmaster, but that is what is happening to me and many more like me. God give us the strength to carry through whatever we set out to do. There is a newspaper, Mary-Anne, called the *Freeman's Journal*, which is very loud in its condemnation of the actions of Britain here in this sad and sorry land. And there is a great man here, a Protestant, by the name of John Mitchel. If you have never heard of him before, you will hear much of him in future. I can remember one of his speeches, in which he said it is stupid to regard the Famine as a 'visitation of Providence' instead of a 'visitation of English landlordism – as great a curse to Ireland as if it was the archfiend himself had the government of the country'. He finished up saying that 'The Almighty, indeed, sent the potato blight, but the English created the Famine'. It is so true for him.

There is another newspaper from across the water, the *Times*, which the Master of this house gets delivered here. I was fortunate to have an opportunity to read it – although misfortunate might be a better word, for it roused an almighty anger in me by suggesting the idea that the Irish Famine, if properly availed of, would prove a great blessing, a valuable opportunity for settling the vexed question of Irish misery and discontent. This paper actually suggested that the 'impecunious Irish tenants' be expelled from the land and replaced by 'thrifty Scotch and scientific English farmers, men with means, who would pay punctually, and not agitate and join secret societies'. Would you credit what else this paper suggested, Mary-Anne? 'In a few more years a Celtic Irishman will be as rare in Connemara as is the Red Indian on the shores of Manhattan.'

A fierce anger raged within me when I finished reading this *Times*. Soon I will join the Young Irelanders, along with the great men who have pledged their lives to the liberation of our small country. One of these men, by name James Fintan Lalor, is of the opinion that landlordism as we have it here should be destroyed, and that the land held by the landlords should be handed back to a 'secure and independent agricultural peasantry'. I heard him myself proclaim: 'Ireland her own, from the sod to the sky, the soil of Ireland for the people of Ireland, to have and hold from God above who gave it.' Stirring words, Mary-Anne. These men were of the same thinking as Daniel O'Connell at first, but he did not go along with their threats of rebellion which, to my mind, were just that – threats and no more.

Last year another organisation named the Irish Confederation came into being following a disagreement. William Smith O'Brien, another Protestant, and Charles Gavan Duffy are other great men who are striving for the betterment of this woeful island. I'll be travelling to Dublin shortly to sign my name. I feel that I will be doing the right thing, but my decision must be my own entirely. God help us, is all I can say.

To other matters...

I do not wish that my letter to you should be of no other interest except political, so I will tell you of other happenings. Our school is struggling, very low in numbers. Lady Anne sees no further need for Miss Phoebe and dispensed with her services last Friday. A high-handed woman is Lady A; she just does what she wants, no real thought for people. What will Miss Phoebe do? Become a governess, maybe. Poor girl, she cried bitter tears on her departure. My Lady gave her a gift of a pearl-backed dressing-table set... No doubt she had not considered that monetary compensation would have been much more agreeable to Miss Chapman.

I am dismayed at this turn of events, as my sewing skills are nil. You will smile at this, Mary-Anne, as no doubt you will recall the many buttons your good mother sewed on for me on the old days. My little girls will have no sewing skills after this either. My little children are in dire distress, and many come to school no more. The soup kitchens are finished – that man Trevelyan is convinced that Ireland's great evil is not 'famine' but the 'selfish, perverse and turbulent character of the people'. He seems more concerned that 'charity will demoralise the Irish than that starvation might kill them'. What manner of man is this? He will face his maker one day, and would that I be there to witness this meeting … You see, Mary-Anne, that I cannot keep away from talking of the bad happenings. You will not want more letters like this from me...

I do not know how long more our school will last. The courage of these poor hungry people constantly amazes me. The children come, as clean as can be possible in the conditions, and try to do their lessons. I wonder at the purpose of teaching reading, writing and arithmetic to children whose lifetime may be just a matter of weeks. The parties in the great house are less frequent now, but whatever leftovers there are, Father O'Beirne puts them to good use. Visitors come and go at the House – no white faces, no bag of bones there, yet I hear the Master complain of shortages. The difference between those who have and those who haven't is surely 'expectation'; whole families would live for a week on one course put up on table in the House.

Time is going slowly, yet it is almost a year since you left Moneen. Are you the same girl yet? Have you changed in yourself? If you have a likeness I would be happy to have it. I now sport a beard as black as my hair, and am more robust than when you saw me last. In my mind and heart I have changed too. I hate injustice, and whereas before I let things pass me by, now I am not so airy-fairy.

Will we ever meet again, Mary-Anne? God alone knows.

Please convey my greetings to your family.

God go with you, *a stóir.*

Seán Thornton.

# CHAPTER 5

## March 15th 1848

HAVING posted his letter to Mary-Anne in the General Post Office, Seán Thornton turned off from Sackville Street at the corner of Abbey Street and proceeded to the Music Hall where the meeting organised by the Young Irelanders was to take place. Dublin was not a city of which he was fond, but he was here for a purpose, and the noise, dirt and size of the capital were not going to deflect him in it in any way.

There was a number of men in the large room to which he was directed. Chairs had been set out in front of the long table at the head of the room. As Seán sat down, a group of men entered from a side door and took their seats behind this table. He immediately recognised one of them, a dark-haired good-looking young man with heavy side-burns, as William Smith O'Brien. The man seated on his left was introduced to the assembly as Thomas Francis Meagher. He was a young man in his early twenties, with a calm steadfast look and piercing dark eyes which swept the assembled men as he stood to acknowledge the intro-duction. Seán recalled hearing of this young man and a fierce speech he had given in favour of armed rebellion at a previous meeting – a speech which had earned him the title of 'Meagher of the Sword'. His passion belied the calm cast of his features.

The meeting was noisy and there were many exchanges between the floor and the podium, but the overall impres-sion was of dedication to the cause. Mr Smith O'Brien invited names from the assembly for service in an armed guard, and he also informed them that an Irish Brigade was to be recruited in the United States. These remarks were greeted with cheers from the gathering.

There was no doubting the sincerity and the high-mindedness of the men in that room. Seán's heart was racing and his mind was filled with wild dreams of working for the freedom of Ireland. He tried to steady himself, maintain his composure, but he was being carried along with the fervour of the crowd. He found himself on his feet, cheering and applauding the men at the table. Smith O'Brien said that he was not anxious for bloodletting; 1782 had been bloodless, and he expected that the rebellion of 1848 would be likewise, in the name of God.

Seán left the Music Hall with his mind in a whirl. He had given in his name, the die was cast... There had been a mention of some sort of disturbance to be organised on St Patrick's Day, two days from now. He was due back in Wexford on the morrow, but as there was to be a mass meeting at the North Wall on the 20th, he decided to defer his return for another few days.

That evening Seán boarded with his friends in the Society of Friends headquarters, but he did not reveal his future plans to them. He felt that these good people would not favour what he was now involved with.

St Patrick's Day passed without any incident, possibly because it was a miserably wet day, and very few people ventured on to the streets. Disappointed, Seán spent the next two days walking the side streets of the city, realising that the main thoroughfares were not indicative of the poverty and desolation which haunted the tenements and shacks of the lanes and alleyways of Dublin. He saw wasted, sickly people, and little children with spindly legs and pinched faces, their hands outstretched, begging for food. He knew that cholera was now rampant throughout these areas. He had seen it all before, and it was not new to him. He had survived before, and he would again. Seeing these dreadful sights only reinforced his determination to succeed with the Young Irelanders in their endeavours for the country.

He walked through Marlborough Street to see once more the house where he had lived with the other trainee teachers in the early 1840s, before eventually getting his first appointment in Moneen. He knew that should his attendance at the Music Hall meeting come to the knowledge of anyone in authority in the National School system, he would be instantly dismissed. The restrictions on the personal freedom of teachers were very tough, and no teacher could take part in politics, attend Repeal meetings, or belong to secret societies.

Seán mused on these points as he made his way back to his base. The rules and regulations of his means of making a living were very restrictive. The salary was very basic, and being paid half-yearly was another burden in itself. Having to mind every penny and stretch such limited resources over many months caused severe problems for many a good master. In many cases of which he was personally aware, the teacher had to use a percentage of his salary to supplement the needs of the school in which he taught.

Two days later Seán attended the meeting at the North Wall. The crowd was large enough, but smaller than what had been expected. Admiration of the courage of the French people was noted, and the necessity to 'address' Her Majesty on the need for an immediate Repeal of the Union was mooted. The meeting passed off quietly and the crowd dispersed without incident.

The following day, boarding the train for his return journey to Wexford, Seán was amazed to hear people discussing the news that O'Brien, Meagher and Mitchel had been summoned by the police. O'Brien and Meagher were charged with 'having made seditious speeches' at the Music Hall meeting, and Mitchel with publishing seditious articles in the *United Irishman*. Seán was glad to hear that they had been given bail and remanded. He felt a shiver pass through him. The arrests had brought home to him the very responsible nature of the venture on which he had embarked.

He travelled back to Ballycromane, hoping that perhaps there would be a letter awaiting him from Mary-Anne. Whether or aye, he was determined that he would begin another letter to her and tell her all the details of this latest episode in his life …

## Letter from Mary-Anne Joyce to Seán Thornton.

## July 1848

Dear Seán,

YOUR letter has reached me safely, and your news was very interesting to Mam, Dad and myself. We are anxious about you and how you fared in the fighting.

But, first of all, you will have been wondering at the delay in hearing from us. Well, our letters have been passing in the Atlantic, Mam says – so I have waited and waited very impatiently for your letter, but now I can reply to you immediately today.

We have had news here about the failure of the rebellion, and the fact that in the end not enough people gave their complete support. We have heard about the final hours in the Widow McCormack's cabbage garden in Ballingarry – were you there? You might like to know that Mam and Dad and myself have been to meetings here and have listened to men like Micheál Doheny, Thomas Darcy McGee and Richard Gorman. No doubt you know of these great men. They told us of John Mitchel being transported to Tasmania, and also of William Smith O'Brien, Thomas Francis Meagher and the others who were also captured and sent to Tasmania. All us Irish love and admire and respect these men, and we will aid them in whatever more they plan to do for the freedom of Ireland.

There is a ballad that Dad and Arthur sing, called

'Revenge for Skibbereen'. Some of the words are 'The day will come when vengeance loud will call, and we will rise with Erin's boys to rally one and all'...

So, Seán, you can know that we are all of the same thinking as yourself, and if I were at home I would be after doing the same thing myself ...

We are doing fine over here, thanks be to God, but as lonely as ever. The Irish here cling close to each other. We speak our language together, dance our dances together, and pray together. It is hard to break away from the old ways, and it is a great consolation to be with our own in a strange land; it keeps us going and the memories of home are forever fresh in our minds.

We have been here now one year and one month; my first birthday in America was my sixteenth. I have put my hair up, and Dad says I am a young lady now. I am sending you a likeness as you asked – you will see very little difference but that my hair is coiled up in my head. People of other countries who live in our area often remark on my red hair. It is a strange colour in this land of mixed races. With the good food I am not so thin any more and have grown up an inch or so.

Dad and Arthur have a second forge now. It is in the Bronx, a way off from here. They are very busy, which is a good thing. Mam and Bina are still sewing for the fine ladies, and me likewise. There is a chance for me to work in one of those fine houses in Gramercy, as a maid to a young lady, to keep her clothes in good order, to dress her hair and to accompany her on outings. Bina met one of the family she worked for years ago and mentioned me, so this week, on Thursday, I go to meet the family.

This is not what I wish to do with myself. Do not even smile when I tell you my real wish. It is to write stories and tales for children and grown-ups. Father O'Rourke, before he returned to Ireland in April, enrolled me in a lending library, and I have been reading in the evenings many, many books... Mam and Dad laugh at me and say,

'You're a dreamer, *a grá*.'

We think it comical that you now have a beard. Would I pass you by, not knowing it is you? No, I don't think so – your eyes can never change their blueness. I'd know you all right.


## July 12th 1848

SEAN, I am now a lady's maid, as from today, and come July 20th I will be living in one of the fine houses – the houses that face on to the park where Mam and me used to walk to see the green grass when we came to New York first.

## July 20th 1848

MARY-ANNE Joyce is now lady's maid to Miss Janine Wiseman. My wage is equal to thirty pounds a year and my keep. The work is hard enough. I rise early and carry the hot water from the scullery for my young miss's morning bath. I wash her clothes, press them and repair them where needed, walk with her through the park, go shopping in the big stores on the main avenues, read to her, sing to her if she is weary, and brush her hair, one hundred strokes morning and night. Miss Janine is a delicate girl; she has a blood condition which does not allow for romping or playing games. Her father is a medical man in the big hospital, and her mother does a great deal of charity work in the slums of New York, of which there are many. Sad to say, many of the people living in these slums are from Ireland. This land has not benefited all who came here ...

Dad has a deal of money put by for a small farm in a country area away from here. He has always been a farmer. Mam would like to return to that life too. She finds the city too noisy and loud and crowded.

What way is life for the people in Ireland now? Are the potatoes coming good this year? Are people still begging on the streets, still living in the hedges and ditches? I still shiver when I remember the way things were for us back in Moneen. Is there any signs of a better living for those who stayed behind? Is there any way we over here can help those at home? If you know any way in which we can be of help, tell us when you write again.

I am wondering what you think of my wish to write. Please give me your advice in your next letter.

Mam and Dad send their greetings to you, our dear friend across the sea.

Love from Mary-Anne.

# CHAPTER 6

## Letter from Seán Thornton to Mary-Anne Joyce.

## August 1848

Mary-Anne,

IT IS a changed man I am since I last took pen to paper to write to you and your family. I was full of fire and enthusiasm then; now I am sad and disillusioned. No letter from my family in New York, and our great rebellion a hopeless gesture. My heart is low.

How are things with you over there? I trust there is no sad news on its way to me. Your letters are my lifeline to the old days. I await to hear, but in the meantime I will tell you of the happenings over the past months.

In my last letter to you, which I hope arrived safely, I gave you news of the Young Irelanders and their great hopes of a rebellion which would gain Ireland the freedom to govern herself, and our people the incentive to be the great race, proud and free, our forefathers were. It was not to be, Mary-Anne. I give you the details as they happened.

When I returned to Ballycromane in late March gone by, I had an uneasy time. Problems in the school, problems in the House. Lady Anne is not a well woman these past months, and has been confined to her room with severe migraine for weeks on end. Attendance at the school is very low; my poor children are struggling, but we carry on as best we can. Miss Jane comes to school on occasion in place of her mother. She is a quiet girl, with not much to say for herself, yet she is kind to the children and very patient with their slowness. I feel it is a matter of time before school closes its doors for lack of pupils.

In the months of May last I made my way to the city of Dublin again, this time for the trial of Mr Smith O'Brien. I was part of the crowd who walked with him from his lodgings in Westland Row to the Law Courts, where the trials are held. It is a great building, with a splendid facade, like many of the buildings in Dublin. It has a granite front and is very impressive indeed. I was glad of the opportunity, however sad, to view the inside of this building. Mr Smith O'Brien was defended by Mr Isaac Butt, a renowned gentleman in law circles here, and he was freed.

The following day I also attended for the trial of Thomas Francis Meagher. The jury was, as they say, 'packed', there being only one Catholic and a single member of the Society of Friends on it. Mr Butt again defended, but the jury found Mr Meagher guilty and sentenced him to fourteen years' transportation. Let me tell you, Mary-Anne, this great man will be sorely missed in this country.

On July 23rd, I went to a further meeting in Enniscorthy, not too far a journey from here. There was not a great turnout, a hundred or so maybe. There was a priest there who warned Mr Smith O'Brien that people were not prepared, either physically or mentally, for fight. Mr Smith O'Brien and his group, myself included, travelled to many villages and towns, trying to encourage people to come out and fight for their freedom. In one or two places we got a great welcome, particularly in Callan in the county of Kilkenny. Even the Royal Irish Hussars, who are stationed there, attended our meeting and were quite friendly towards us. After Callan we went on to the town of Carrick-on-Suir, and there hundreds turned out to welcome us. We rested there, our horses – and ourselves as well – needing food and drink. There was a meagre supply of arms there, mainly pikes, which are not of much value against muskets. When rested we proceeded on to Cashel of the Kings. This town is noted for its magnificent ruins of Cormac's Chapel, high in a hill overlooking the town. It is a sight to behold, Mary-Anne. Sadly, not one person turned out to aid us, and we pushed further on towards Killenaule, and then Mullinahone, but only a handful greeted us there.

However, the chapel bells were tolled and by late that night a crowd of maybe six thousand had gathered. There was much activity about the place. Pikes were hammered out in the local forges, and all was fire and fervour. However, towards morning, the men came looking for food, of which there was next to nothing. To our eternal shame, we had neglected to provide for these hungry people. Mr Smith O'Brien did his best to give some sustenance, but the crowds began to drift away. I believe that many came in the first instance hoping there would be some food available.

This same story was repeated in the next village, and the next, and at the end of the week, on the Saturday, only a bare handful, myself included, remained. We were badly armed and weary, and as a consequence, the rebellion was dying on its feet.

We ended up in the townsland of Ballingarry, next to the house of a widow-woman, a Mrs McCormack, who was the sole support of a large family. The police barricaded themselves inside the house, and as it was not possible to confront them with comparable weapons, it was decided to try to smoke them out of the place. The Widow McCormack got into a state and began to screech and roar, and search for the children. Some shots were fired from inside the house and two of our gallant few fell dead. The shot passed close to my head. I was lucky. It is heartbreaking to see two men, who had been full of life one minute, cold and dead the next. I can say that we did our best, but I know now that the time was not right, and that lack of food was the major factor in the failing of our rising. I did not agree with Mr Smith O'Brien when he said afterwards: 'It matters little whether the blame of failure lies on me or on others, but the fact is recorded in our annals that the people preferred to die of starvation at home, or to flee as voluntary exiles to other lands, rather than to fight for their lives and liberties.' To my mind hunger clouds vision, and food to fill an empty belly is the most important thing to a hungry man. Those of us with full bellies did not give enough thought to those without. I have seen sorry sights in Tipperary too, and I feel shame for expecting these poor, hungry and deprived people to follow someone else's dream …

Mary-Anne, I have been doing a lot of thinking about my future here in Ireland. I believe that my teaching life is nearing a crisis. My pupils are leaving one by one, some to die, and it is a fact that school and learning are of little benefit presently. The harvest of this year is as bad as 1845 and 1846, and the potato crop a disaster. We had high hopes after last year's great results, but the blight has struck again, even worse than before. The city of Dublin is devastated by cholera, and there is fear that it will spread further afield. Even the wealthy are not immune to this awful disease. I have come to the decision that I will travel to the United States as soon as I can acquire a passage …

## September 1848

MARY-ANNE, I have spoken to Lady Anne and advised her of my plans. She is of course ignorant of my part in the rebellion, and it is as well that she remain so. She had a suggestion for me: her husband was in need of a book-keeper for a short few weeks, and she asked me if I would be agreeable to remain on in their employ for that time. She also remarked, with quite a deal of embarrassment, that her daughter had a fondness for me and would possibly fret herself into a decline were I to leave immediately.

Mary-Anne, you will understand that I was very shaken

when she informed me of this turn of events. I have spoken to Miss Jane only on rare occasions, such as when she has come to the school in her mother's absence, and I have never given her any encouragement in any way. I will endeavour to avoid this young girl in so far as is possible, and when she is finally released from the schoolroom she will develop friendships with her own age-group. I said as much to her mother, who, I am surprised to say, agreed with me, going on to say that young ladies who are educated at home and cosseted a great deal quite often form attachments for any young unattached man in their vicinity. 'A passing phase,' she assured me. I earnestly hope this is true.

## October 1848

YOUR letter has come. Your likeness is on my table as I write, and indeed your father is right. Mary-Anne is now a young lady with coiled-up hair, soft eyes and a gentle smile. No longer the tomboy who clambered over the hills and waded in the streams, who climbed trees and tickled the trout from the river bank. America has changed the girsheen *brea* into a young lady, yet I can see traces of the Mary-Anne who loves Ireland as I do.

God knows what the future holds for us, *a stóir*, but if all my plans work out, you and I will meet again, perhaps in the not too distant future.

I am glad to hear of your plans to write stories. It is something you have a natural leaning towards, and I am confident you will succeed in this venture.

Your friend, Seán Thornton.

# CHAPTER 7

**Letter from Mary-Anne Joyce to
Seán Thornton.**

**November 1848**

Dear Seán,

IT IS evening time here in New York. The days are short now; it is winter time and it is very cold. I am writing this 'story' to you in my bedroom in the attic of this great house in which I am now living. I will try to describe this house to you. It is a high house, with three floors above the basement. There are eight steps up to the front door, with railings each side of these steps. Each morning Matilda, the scullery maid, has to scrub and scrub them until they are white. The main entrance door is massive, way, way above my head, and it has brasses and a bell-push. There are two long windows each side of the door, and five windows on each level above. There is an entrance below the steps which is used by the servants to enter and leave the house. At the rear of the building there is a double gate which leads into a courtyard, the coach house, the stables and the gardens. The tradesmen also use these gates to make their deliveries to the main house.

There are so many rooms in this big house. I have been in but a few of them, except for the kitchens, Miss Janine's apartments, and my own sleeping quarters in the attic. The day I came here to meet Mr and Mrs Wiseman I was shown into the front reception room through the first door on the left from the main hallway. There were so many chairs, tables, lamps and ornaments in the room that I was afraid to move, afeared that I would break something or fall over some piece of furniture. The chairs were large and of leather, the tables and cabinets shiny and polished. The curtains of dark red velvet were held back with tassels of the same colour. I had a good look around me at all the objects and ornaments. I hoped to remember as much as I could so I would be able to tell you of the riches here in this house. There are so many poor people living but a block away.

The entrance hall of this house is as big as a room, with a polished wooden floor. There are two doors on each side, and at the back a stairway rises up to the next floor. To the back of the first steps there is a curtain and behind that, as I now know, is the doorway leading to the kitchens. There are many framed paintings on the walls and the stairway. When Miss Janine is eighteen her likeness will be painted and will hang in the hallway also.

I will tell you about my day. I rise every morning at six, wash and ready myself. I must wear a uniform, which is a black dress high to the neck, and down to the top of my boots. Over this I wear a white apron with a frill all around it. My hair is held back in a coil and I wear a lace cap which is caught with hairpins to the top of my hair. My hands have never been so clean, and all the hard bits have been well softened, seeing as I am over two years away from working on the land. Miss Janine gave me lotions to put on my hands and for my face to keep the freckles as few as possible. Mam and Dad say they love my freckles, they go with my colour hair. I have a tallboy in my room, and over it there is a looking-glass, so I can see how I look before I go to her room in the mornings.

I carry the cans of hot water to Miss Janine's room on the second floor, and fill her bath, which is placed close to the fire, already lit by Matilda a half hour or more before. After the bathing I help Miss Janine to dress, and then brush her hair and set it for the daytime and in readiness for breakfast, which I fetch from the kitchens. So much running up and down the stairs – I had pains in my legs when I first began this work. I'll be well set for the hills and mountains when I go home to Galway.

Miss Janine is a delicate girl and cannot take part in any active games. She likes to drive her pony and carriage through the large park some distance from her home. I sit beside her, and a groom sits at the rear, and we have many a pleasant afternoon's outing in the fine weather. She named her pony Beauty, and I do think of my little grey donkey back home, whose ears I would scratch, and the sadness comes over me often.

## December 1848

IT IS some days since I began this 'story' to you. I went to see Mam and Dad yesterday. They are well and content now that they have found the small farm which they hope to buy. It is up towards the Catskill mountains and they expect to be living there a few months from now. Bina and Arthur called in to see me, knowing that I was on my hours off, and they too plan to move out of the city and into the country. There is no look of worry or strain on their faces now. The fact that in a short time they will be leaving the crowded city has given each of them a look of contentment and peace. They ask me if I wish to go with them. I do not know yet.

My own face still bears what Mam says is a 'question mark'. Bina agrees with her, and she said to me, 'When you have your heart's desire the question mark will be gone forever.' I go about my work happily but there is a pain somewhere inside me, and a need to go back home to Galway, to see the purple mountains, to breathe the clear air of Ireland. The pain never goes away. Here I am, going on three years in this land, and yet I am only half here. I walk and I talk and I laugh, but it seems that a part of me stands aside all the time. Can you understand?

Seán, your letter came to hand today. I am amazed at

the turn of events you describe. The failure of the rebellion was a disappointment, no doubt, but the seeds it sowed will blossom forth in a future generation. It is not a lost cause. You did what you had to do.

Mr Isaac Butt is a remarkable man. Is it not strange how, from unconsidered sources, great men come? John Mitchel too. His was a severe sentence for a sincere man; history will prove the real judge in his case. I think that Mr Smith O'Brien is also a remarkable person, very strong in his mind, and, it would seem, hard driven by his own strong ideals.

Cholera strikes fear in my heart. God keep you safe from that terrible scourge.

I am in two minds about you taking the boat to America – for selfish reasons. When I think of home and Ireland I think of you, both bound together in my mind ...

## January 1849

Dear Seán,

WE have passed through Christmas time and into a new year. There is deep snow here in the city, and it is difficult to travel any distance on foot. The sleighs travel so easy over the packed snow. Miss Janine has harnessed Beauty to the sleigh and we bowl along nicely. The days are clear, bright and so very cold. We wear heavy coats and hats on our outings; my old black shawl would be out of place here, but it would surely keep the heat in me, and Mamo's knitted *cáibín* would be well used by me in this wintry world.

When we came back from our outing yesterday the groom, seeing that it was snowing heavily, drew up at the front of the house so that Miss Janine and I could enter by the main door. When Miss Janine was changing from her outdoor clothes we discovered that one of her gloves was missing. I hastened to recover it from the street. As I descended the steps I heard someone whistling 'The Rakes of Mallow'. I stopped, believing I was imagining things, but no, it was 'The Rakes of Mallow', and it was being whistled by a policeman who was sheltering from the falling snow by the lower door.

When he saw me he stopped his whistling and said, 'Isn't it a fierce cold day?' I could hardly believe it, and just stood and stared at him. Then he said, as plain as day, 'With your red hair you have to be Irish.'

Mam has always warned me against conversing with strangers, but I felt it would be unmannerly to ignore him, so I said, 'Yes, I am from Ireland.'

Then he said, 'Aye, the same as myself. I have seen you coming and going, and now's my chance to speak with you.' Having recovered Miss Janine's glove, I should have hastened indoors from the heavy snow, but I stayed a while longer and we spoke about home and what is happening there. He gave his name as Timothy O'Connor, from Kerry, and he has been in New York for five years. He plans, when he has money, to return to Ireland again. He says his beat is around Gramercy Avenue and that he will watch out for me another time.

When I returned indoors Miss Janine remarked on my red cheeks. The cold made them red, I told her.

I borrow from the Lending Library every week, and I read chapters from a book every day, sometimes reading aloud for Miss Janine. She has given me permission to use her dictionary to discover the meanings of strange words. So my English language is improving steadily, and soon I will endeavour to write stories for children.

A pleasant and happy thought has come to me. I may *see* you before your next letter comes to me.

Mam and Dad always ask to be remembered to you.

I am, my dear Master Thornton, your friend, Mary-Anne.

# CHAPTER 8

SEÁN had almost completed the accounts for Lord Salford-Broone, and he planned to travel to Clare and visit his home place before travelling to America. His position in the Salford-Broone family had become a little uncomfortable in recent times. Miss Jane, a gentle, quiet girl who blushed whenever he encountered her, had taken to meeting him by chance on his daily walk around the gardens, and to appearing at the library door on some pretext or other during his working hours, and all in all he did not wish to encourage her in any way. He endeavoured to speak pleasantly to her whenever he could – not to avoid a meeting, but because he was beginning to feel out of patience with his position in the household.

As soon as he decently could, he would leave and go home to Clare to see for himself how things were. News still filtered through of evictions, disease and destruction in the West. People there had been entirely dependent on the potato, and following the black harvest of the previous year, there was simply nothing left to keep life in them. Mr Trevelyan was once again causing heartbreak. The previous September he had made public that Treasury grants to the hard-pressed unions were to finish. He apparently believed the people to be too dependent on Government aid, and therefore to further 'encourage' the people to be more independent, he decided to stop feeding the forlorn and destitute children. It was also a belief of the same Mr Trevelyan that the emigration of the fairly 'comfortable' farmer was a good thing. 'I do not know how farms are to be consolidated if small farmers do not emigrate, we must not complain of what we really want to obtain,' was his sentiment as printed in the *Times*. He expressed the desire 'that the landlords be induced to sell portions of their estates to persons who would invest capital which would prove a satisfactory settlement of Ireland'.

Just a few days before, Seán had received another letter, from Mary-Anne. He had been anxious about her reaction to his plan to emigrate to the United States. He had a vague sense of disquiet about her possible response, as her desire to return to Ireland permeated her every letter to him. No kith or kin of her own remained in the bleakness which was Connacht. If he himself were absent, whom would she have when she returned?

Poor Ireland – even the landlords and the gentry were being ruined by high rates and no rents from the vacant holdings of the dead and the emigrated. What hope for others if the 'gentry' were not able to withstand the harsh and unjust demands of an absentee Government? Seán believed that the United States had gained so much, unwittingly, from the Famine. The farmers who should be farming in Ireland were now using their expertise in another country, for the betterment of that land and people. Poor, desolate Ireland, he thought, what hope has she?

## February 1849

SEÁN had finished his packing, and now he made his way to the morning room to made his farewells to the Salford-Broone family. He was now ready to travel back to Clare for a short visit before taking the *Cushlamachree* from Galway in April. The family were seated, Lady Anne busy with her embroidery frame, the master with his *Times*, and Miss Jane with arranging flowers. He bade his farewells and was astonished when he was presented with a leather-bound volume of the works of Shakespeare by his Lordship and Lady Anne, and some hemstitched handkerchiefs from Miss Jane. For a brief instance he was aware of the innate goodness of these people and he regretted that he had never tried really to understand them and their way of life. He expressed his sincere gratitude for their gifts and was assured that there would always be a welcome for him should he ever wish to pay a call on them.

As he was driven down the avenue he turned to look at Cromane House for the last time, and reflected that yet another phase of his life had come to an end. What more was ahead of him?

## March 1849

SUCH desolation, such beggary, dirt and disease. Seán was heartbroken at the scenes he encountered on his long journey home to Clare. Since Trevelyan had ordered the cessation of food for the children, the evidence of his inhuman act was visible all through the country. Little yellow-faced creatures, many with peculiar hair growths on their bodies, and with the bones of their spindly legs and bodies almost visible. Crammed workhouses, naked people crawling the roads, dead bodies left where they had fallen.

Asiatic cholera was now raging throughout the country. There were no funds available to provide even the most basic care. It seemed to Seán that there was no longer any sympathy for Ireland and her misfortunes. It was as if the world were fed up with problems of this poor little country, and had completely lost interest.

The attempted insurrection of the previous spring had roused the ire of the Government, and Ireland was going to have to pay a severe price for daring to show dissatisfaction with British rule.

# March 1849

SEÁN made his way down the boreen, passing the empty homes of neighbours and finally reaching the cottage where he had been born and bred. He rested his arms on the crumbling wall and gazed his fill at his old home, resting in the shade of trees planted many years before by his grandfather. No one had lived in the cottage since his mother had passed away in 1843, never to know the misery of the Famine. He pressed his way through the overgrown garden, the nettles and briars combining to bar his way. He pulled back the half-door, pressed the rusty latch and, with a great deal of effort, managed to creak open the door.

It took a minute or so for his eyes to get accustomed to the dark of the inside. He found his way to the window and brushed away the dirt and cobwebs to let a little light through. The room, the kitchen, in which he stood had once been the centre of his life. He looked around, searching for familiar things. The hearth was festooned with twigs of long-discarded crows' nests, the crane still held a rusted kettle, and the hobs were inches deep in dust and grime. There was the remains of a bed in the outshot, and, in the 'bowl' in the wall above it, his searching fingers found a horse's bit, the pipe once treasured by his father and a medal.

Seán gazed up at the ceiling, at the sods well blackened by smoke, and at the furze strips and the oaken crossbeams, crudely shaped, taken from the bog many years before, when the cottage was being built. Seán remembered his grandfather telling him the story of these beams, how they had lain beneath the bog, under layers of overgrowth, for centuries. Their position could be located by the fact that the dew or frost never rested on the ground below which they lay, and these places were duly marked out for excavation by the craftsmen. He touched the beams, running his fingers along their length, wondering at the age of them. Probably they were thousands of years old. His grandfather had shown him the wooden pegs holding these massive beams in place, and told him how holes had been burned in the beams and the wooden pegs inserted at a slant and hammered into place, to last hundreds of years.

Seán climbed into the loft and the tears finally came when he found the fiddle which his grandfather had passed on to him when his rheumaticky fingers could no longer ply the bow or finger the strings. He stood in the kitchen and sobbed out loud, crying for the happy times of his boyhood in this house, for his parents and sister, for the terrible waste of life in his land.

Seán dried his eyes, feeling somehow that all the pressure of the past years had been relieved by this outburst of grief. He took another long look around him, wishing to imprint on his mind the reminders of his boyhood: the old dresser, the spinning wheel, the ancient chair by the hearth, the wall lamp still in place on its hook. He looked into the other room, now containing just the old cupboard and the table where the butter had been kept away from the heat of the kitchen. The pull-down bed was no more, and the bare floor bore much evidence of the presence of mice.

Seán closed the door carefully behind him, drew the top of the half-door fast, looked around him for the last time, and then blessed himself and walked away.

# CHAPTER 9

**March 1849**

**Letter from Seán Thornton to
Mary-Anne Joyce.**

Dear Mary-Anne,

I AM leaving Ireland in two weeks and will travel to the
United States on the *Cushlamachree*, sailing out from
Galway, in April. The decision has not been an easy one. I
have this terrible feeling that I am betraying the poor
starving people by going away and leaving them in their
agony. When I spoke to Father Byrne about going away
and about my concern as to whether it was right thing to
do. he said to me, 'Go to America, Seán, you could do a
lot of good over there. The task here is beyond us. Go and
get help for us from our people over there.' I have had life
easy since leaving Moneen, living in comfort in a house
which knew no shortages, so I have a fair bit of strength
left, but for how long more?

I am hungry, Mary-Anne. Even as I write this letter,
there is half a turnip and a can of spring water to feed me
for the few days remaining here in Clare. Father Byrne
has allowed me to lodge in his house, along with many
more worse off than me.

I went to my old home for a last look before I go away,
and my heart nigh broke. Memories of my childhood, my
boyhood – they washed over me and I was hard put to
walk away from all that I hold dear.

Your last letter was read with great interest. Mary-
Anne, your new life seems to be a contented one. It is
good to hear that your parents have realised their dream to

farm again. Have you given any thought to going with them to live in the Catskill mountains?

The prospect of thirty to forty days on board ship is something I put to the back of my mind. However, the stories coming back to Ireland of the awful crossings, the deaths, the ill treatment, infectious diseases, and, worse, the way our people are being so badly treated even by those gone before them and settled, makes me despair at times. Surely Irish people should help their countrymen newly arrived in the United States? Have you had any experience of this?

It is truly amazing, the good work done by so many on behalf of the poor and needy people. The weather here has been cold and frosty, so Father Byrne decided to help people to raise money so that they can at least buy meal to eat. Turf can be taken into the town by donkey carts and sold for small money, and the empty bellies can be filled even if only for a short time. The priest is trying to get the people working all day, thus ensuring that the cartloads of turf brought in to the town will see regular amounts of money, small though they be, in the hands of the needy. However, Mary-Anne, the Father says that motivating people to continue this method of earning money is not easy. For some reason the people have a dislike of trading, as if it is something to be ashamed of. He shakes his head at the foolhardiness of those who splurge their small earnings and then must do without until they sell more turf.

There has been some benefit in the Galway area with the Shannon Improvements scheme in '47. Many of the people who were employed under the scheme showed they could work well. The use of this river is not fully exploited as of yet, but in years to come it will prove most beneficial.

Mary-Anne, there is such a void here between those who have and those who have not. I know men who would work their fingers to the bone given half the chance. The pity of it is that other lands will have the benefits of their industry. The poor have hunger, hovels and disease; the rich have great houses, idleness and stupid pride. There is no 'in between' the two and I cannot see how this chasm of difference can ever be breached.

It is hard to be light-hearted in Ireland as it is at present. When I read back over this letter to you, Mary-Anne, I am hard put not to throw it in the fire. It is full of despondency and trouble, but it is well nigh impossible for it to be other than that, in the circumstances. Please forgive me for my dismal 'writings', and keep poor old Ireland in your prayers.

This letter will precede me by about two weeks. It will go out from Limerick, so you will know ahead of time when I am due to reach New York, and I look forward with great happiness to meeting with you, your good parents and the old neighbours once again.

Your friend, Seán Thornton.

# CHAPTER 10

## April 1849

MARY-ANNE lay on her narrow bed high in the attic room of 39-30 Gramercy Avenue, reading the letter from Seán which had been delivered that morning.

She was so looking forward to seeing Master Thornton. Three years had gone by since she had last seen him – three long, lonely years – but now the waiting was over, and with her mam and dad she would be meeting him off the boat when it docked. She wondered whether he would have changed much from her last memory of the tall, thin and clean-shaven young man who had seen them off on their long journey to this land of great promise. She tried to visualise his face but had some difficulty doing so. For an instant, panic filled her mind. What would happen if they did not recognise each other? Her mam and dad would surely recognise him. She felt little excited shivers dancing through her ...

A sound filtered into her excited mind from below on the street, a sound of whistling. It was 'The Rakes of Mallow'. She leaned into the window, trying vainly to see down to the street below. She wondered whether to go down the stairs, open the door and take a look outside. Stanley, the butler, would certainly ask questions of her if she attempted to do such a thing. She fretted around the room, still hearing the tuneful sound and imagining that it could possibly be Tim O'Connor, the policeman whom she had met by chance some weeks ago.

There had been no opportunity to go outdoors lately, as Miss Janine had been unwell for some time. As her companion, Mary-Anne was expected to keep her company, and this left her with very little free time to herself. The spring weather and the brightening days had, however, brought about an improvement in the young lady's condition. Mary-Anne expected that in a short time their trips out of doors would recommence.

The whistling faded away into the distance...

The bell on the wall above her head jangled loudly. Mary-Anne slipped off the bed and put on her house slippers. Her presence was obviously needed, even though she was on her 'hours off'. She tided her hair, slipped on a fresh apron and smoothed the counterpane free of wrinkles. She put Seán's letter into her handkerchief box, along with all the others from him, and, closing the bedroom door, quietly descended by the back stairs to the rooms occupied by her charge.

'Come in, do,' a faint voice answered her knock. Mary-Anne entered the little sitting room where Miss Janine occasionally rested since she had become ill.

'Mary-Anne, my head aches so badly,' the fretful voice quavered. 'Do give me a massage, you know how it helps me.'

'Of course, Miss,' Mary-Anne said. 'Come into your bedroom and I will prepare the oils.'

Mary-Anne helped the fragile, fair-haired girl up from the *chaise-longue* and, keeping her arm around her waist, assisted her into the bedroom and on to the high, canopied bed facing the window.

'Lie there and get yourself nice and cosy,' Mary-Anne said. 'Shall I put the comforter over you?' At the murmured 'Please', Mary-Anne tucked the fleecy quilt around her charge.

In the silence of the bedroom Mary-Anne carefully blended lavender and marjoram oils into the base oil as Dr Wiseman had instructed her, and carried the bowl through to the bedroom and laid it on the night table beside the bed. She tided back Miss Janine's hair with a pretty ribbon and began to smooth the mixture of oils on to her forehead and temples.

Dr Wiseman was a great believer in natural medicines, and he spent many hours in his apothecary room on the lower floor making up liniments and potions from herbs, plants and flowers. These were grown for the most part in the gardens at the rear of the house. His daughter had had the immense benefit of his excellent success in this area.

'How are you feeling today?' Mary-Anne asked, stroking gently and watching the rather tense face begin to relax and the breathing become easier.

'Quite a deal better, thank you, but it is so slow,' sighed her 'patient'. 'I would wish to hurry up – but Father says it will be some days yet before I may even consider leaving the house.'

'Spring is here,' Mary-Anne said. 'The days are getting warmer. It is the most pleasant time of year, is it not? We will go to the park, maybe next week, to see the spring flowers and plants. You'd like that.'

'Poor Beauty,' Miss Janine murmured. 'She has not had much exercise lately, and I am afraid she will have forgotten me. Do animals forget people, do you think, Mary-Anne?'

'Of course not,' Mary-Anne replied. 'Not at all... Beauty will know you instantly.'

Miss Janine smiled happily. 'I think I will sleep for a while now, Mary-Anne. My head feels so much better.'

Mary-Anne patted off the surplus oil, rearranged the pillows and tucked the comforter in around the drowsy girl.

'Have a nice sleep,' she said, 'and I will wake you around five o'clock with some hot chocolate.'

Closing the bedroom door behind her, Mary-Anne crossed the landing and looked out the window which fronted on to the street below. She had a clear view of the length of it for several blocks. The traffic at that time of day was sparse – a tradesman's wagon, a landau with its front half removed in deference to the lovely spring day, and a brougham, with its unseen passenger, clipped smartly by.

The horses were in fine fettle, and the people on the far sidewalk walked with great lift in their steps too.

'I'll go for a short walk,' Mary-Anne spoke aloud. 'It is seldom a day like this should be missed.'

She knew her charge would sleep for at least an hour following the massage, and there would be plenty of time for a walk and time to prepare supper before Miss Janine would be awake and ready to eat.

Mary-Anne went back upstairs to her room to put on her outdoor clothes and boots. She put her purse into her reticule, as she needed to purchase writing paper at the store on the next street. On her way down she checked on her charge, finding her sleeping peacefully.

'I am going out to make some purchases,' Mary-Anne informed Stanley, the family butler, in reply to his query as to her purpose for leaving the house.

'Very well, Miss, be back within the hour.' Stanley had taken an interest in Mary-Anne from her very first day working for the Wiseman family. In fact, he had set himself up as something of a guardian to her, so Mary-Anne did not resent in any way his questioning of her intentions. 'Make sure you keep to the main thoroughfares, and do not travel through the run-down areas, Miss,' he cautioned her.

'Yes, Stanley, I will be very careful,' Mary-Anne reassured him with a smile.

Bidding him goodbye, she stepped on to the street. Mary-Anne had not admitted to herself the real reason that she was leaving the house for a walk. Granted, she did need writing paper, and she did need fresh air, and she also liked to watch the fashionable people as they strolled the avenues and streets on their constitutional promenade. However, when she observed the tall figure of the policeman approaching as she turned into Wyndham Street, she knew, that having heard his whistling earlier, she had a wish to meet Tim O'Connor again.

'Well, if is isn't Miss Mary-Anne Joyce,' Tim O'Connor remarked as he drew up alongside her, 'and where might you be going this fine day?'

Mary-Anne could feel her face reddening as she stopped beside him. 'Good afternoon, Mr O'Connor,' she said primly. 'I am going to do some shopping.'

'Oh, shopping, are you? Would you be going my way by any chance?'

'I am going over to Sernberg Street, so I do not think that it is on your way.' She smiled a little at him.

'I'm going off duty in ten minutes,' Tim said. 'When you are going back along Wyndham Street I will watch out for you.' He saluted her gravely and stepped smartly on his way.

A faint echo of 'The Rakes of Mallow' drifted back to Mary-Anne as she resumed her walk. In the store she purchased the writing paper and some sewing silk, and wandered around admiring the various items on display. She saw some pretty embroidered handkerchiefs which she knew her mam would like, and some tobacco for her dad. Carrying her packages, she started on her way back to Gramercy Avenue.

TIM O'Connor watched her as she approached. She had not seen him yet, as she was occupied with the comings and goings of people and vehicles – this was a much busier thoroughfare than Gramercy Avenue. He observed the glints of red-gold hair escaping from the snood, the sparkling of freckles across her nose, her upright carriage and her clear Irish complexion, and stepped forward to meet her. When he barred her way she gave a startled cry.

''Tis only me, Mary-Anne Joyce. I didn't mean for to frighten you,' Tim apologised. 'May I walk a way with you?

'I am not sure,' Mary-Anne said primly. 'I don't really know you, and my mother wishes me to be wary of strangers.'

'And quite right she is too,' Tim laughed. 'Sure don't you know me well? Amn't I as Irish as yourself, and a respectable member of the New York police? What more could your mother want?'

Mary-Anne had to laugh herself. Sure what harm would it be if she did walk a way with him?

'And how are you liking the great city of New York?' Tim asked her as they strolled along. 'It's a far cry from a village in Ireland, isn't it?'

'Oh, I like it fine, you know,' Mary-Anne replied. 'I won't be staying forever, you see. I'll be going back to live in Galway again some day.'

'Oh, they all say that,' Tim scoffed. 'All us Irish want to go back home, but things don't always happen the way we'd like. Sure there are terrible happenings over there still. I do be reading in the papers. It'd put the heart cross-ways in you when you read of some of the diseases and the fever madness.'

'I do get letters from the schoolmaster back at home,' Mary-Anne told him, 'so I know the way things are over there, but please God it won't always be like that.'

'So you get letters from a schoolmaster? Well, well, how come he writes to you and not to your mam and dad? Why would an old man be writing to a young one like yourself?' Tim wondered to himself why he was so put out at the idea of Mary-Anne corresponding with another man.

Mary-Anne was a little taken aback but answered, 'He is really very young – he came to teach in our school when the old Master passed away. He asked me to write and tell him how things are with us, and about life in America, so that's what I do. He is coming to live here in about two weeks, so he is.'

'Oh he is, is he?' Tim teased. 'Well, maybe I'll come across him sometime. Himself and meself are probably about the one age.'

They had reached the corner of Gramercy and Wyndham. As Mary-Anne prepared to go back to the house, Tim asked in a casual tone if she often went

78

shopping on her own.

'No, not often. I do be kept busy most of the time, or Miss Janine might need me to accompany her to the stores. Why do you ask?'

She noticed that Tim O'Connor, the pride of the New York police department, was quite nervous and kept shifting from one foot to the other.

'I was wonderin',' he began, 'I was wonderin' – would you wish to walk out with me?' He ended in a rush, and proceeded to gaze into the distance as though his life depended on it.

Mary-Anne could not think of a thing to say.

'Well?' Tim asked. 'Do you have an answer for me at all?'

'You'll have to ask my father about that, Mr O'Connor,' Mary-Anne began. 'You'd need his permission ...?'

'I understand that part of it,' Tim said, 'and I am prepared to ask for his permission to walk out with his daughter. What I really want to know is if *you* want to.' He stopped and regarded Mary-Anne seriously. 'And, please, my name is Tim.'

Mary-Anne looked at him, at his dark eyes, brown wavy hair and pleasant face, and thought: I like him, he is so happy and carefree ... 'Yes, Tim, I would like to walk out with you,' she smiled, 'if my father is in agreement.'

She was entirely unprepared for Tim's loud 'Hooray' and the way he lifted her clean off her feet and twirled her around and around. Her bonnet fell off, her hair came adrift from its pins, and her packages landed in the street. His laughter was contagious and she had to join in. Passers-by gave them amused glances, and, when he finally put her down, Mary-Anne, a little flustered, tried to recover her dignity, her bonnet and her packages.

Dusting herself down, she said, 'I must hurry, I promised Stanley I would be no more than an hour away.'

'Good day to you, Miss Mary-Anne Joyce, and if you

will kindly give me directions to your father's house, I will put my case before him.' Tim O'Connor's eyes were gleaming with merriment as he held his notebook at the ready. Mary-Anne gave him the number of the house and the street and then moved away, quickly hurrying the last block home.

She was still pink with excitement when she arrived; Stanley greeted her and remarked at how fresh she looked. The outdoors was well suited to her, he said. There had been no sound from Miss Janine's room, and her afternoon tea was laid ready in the kitchen...

# Part Three:
## AMERICA

# CHAPTER 11

THE *Cushlamachree* sailed into New York harbour, her graceful lines and billowing sails giving a truly pleasant appearance.

Mary-Anne, her mother and her father were able to observe the tall ship from their vantage point near to the arrivals hall. The three of them were in a high state of excitement as they awaited the arrival of Seán Thornton. But the sight of the poor, bedraggled people filing into the receiving station, some unable to walk and carried in the arms or on the strong backs of relatives, was dreadful. Mary-Anne cried quietly to herself. Though her own voyage to the new world had been three years ago, the picture of the misery before her was too close to her own memories of her ordeal. Such a fine ship, she thought, but such a miserable, weary human cargo coming from its holds. There were hundreds of people there. How would herself and her parents know or recognise Seán?

She clutched her mother's hand tightly. 'Oh, Mam, what if he isn't on board?'

'Of course he is, *a grá*, just keep looking. We'll find him all right,' her mother said. 'You watch to the left, Dad will look to the right and I will watch the middle line.'

Mary-Anne's eyes were dazzled by the shifting moving mass of people, laden down with boxes and baggage. It would be impossible to pick out any one person, but still she strained her eyes, trying to find Seán in the melée.

Then her dad shouted, 'There he is, there he is, over there.'

'Where, where?' Mary-Anne cried. 'Show him to me quick, Dad.'

Her dad brought his head down to her level and pointed. 'Look, just over there. See the tall man carrying the black trunk? Can you see him?'

At last, Mary-Anne had her first sight of Seán Thornton in three years. She saw a tall, bearded man, slightly stooped under the weight of the heavy box which he was balancing on one shoulder. She gazed at him until her eyes gradually adjusted and she could see some resemblance to the man who had been her teacher for a time back home in Ireland.

Jamesy Joyce held high the notice with 'The Joyce Family for Seán Thornton' printed in large black lettering, and waved it to and fro.

SEAN Thornton wearily shifted the heavy wooden box on his shoulder and steadied it with his two hands. He felt so strange and bereft in this crowded hall. As he looked around him for some sight of a familiar face, his attention was caught by the wildly waving notice. He breathed a sigh of intense relief and began to push his way through the throng, gradually edging in the direction of the fluttering sign. As he neared it he recognised Jamesy Joyce, Honor and – it had to be – Mary-Anne. This tall girl, with copper-coloured hair and dancing eyes? My God, she was a young lady now, a far cry from the half-starved, tear-stained child of three years ago.

Seán shifted his box on to the ground and was embraced by Honor, and clapped on the back and had his hand shaken heartily by Jamesy. When he turned to Mary-Anne, she only smiled shyly at him. Then, recovering herself, she threw her arms around him and said, 'Oh, Seán, Master Thornton, we are so happy to have you here. Welcome to America.'

LATER that evening, as they all sat around the table, the questions flew thick and fast. There was so much talking to be done. 'How are things at home?' 'How were the praties this year?' 'What is the weather like now?' 'Is there any sign of a change for the better at all?'

Seán did his best to answer each question. The Joyces were hungry for every bit of news from home. Other neighbours living in the house came by in ones and twos to see the 'Master', and there was much handshaking and back-slapping and not a few tears as people got word of those left behind.

There were angry murmurs as Seán described the awful happenings in Ireland – the epidemic diseases, the way the Unions had collapsed, how the one in Clifden had gone bankrupt so that the people were thrown out and left to fend for themselves. The Government was even more insistent that the rates be collected and that full force was to be used to the verge of the law – and beyond if necessary. Houses were still being 'tumbled' all over the country. He told them of the news filtering in from other counties. Mayo was suffering very badly: houses were being knocked down, and the few possessions of the people dumped in the mud and dirt regardless. In most cases troops were used to drive out the people – troops with not a kind heart amongst them.

Seán told them that some of the Poor Law Inspectors were humane people who did the best they could with the limited means available to them. He related to them the stories of the assassinations of many landlords, and in particular that of Major Mahon of Strokestown in the county of Roscommon. It happened in November of '47, as Mahon was travelling back from a meeting of the Guardians of the Roscommon Union where he had been trying to keep the workhouse open. Bonfires were lit on the rising ground as the people exulted at the news of his death. Terrible times for all, and there were many worse than Major Mahon, it had to be said. The people in the room heartily agreed.

The room by now was full of smoke and fervour. To lighten the atmosphere Jamesy produced the bottle of poteen which he had been saving for such an occasion. There was a taste for all the men – though the women all refused – then someone produced a fiddle and someone else a *feadóg*, and a squeezebox was taken from beneath a shawl. The seats were pushed back, and the people took to the floor for sets and reels and jigs. There was a great to-do, and much cheering and clapping as the feeling of 'being at home', even for a short while, pervaded the room. It was as though outside the door of this high tenement on the east side of New York City, the hills, mountains, rivers and streams of Ireland were waiting. The Joyces and their friends, for a few short hours, forgot the miles which separated them from their home, from their previous lives, and were caught in a happy dream for this short space of time.

# CHAPTER 12

IT WAS arranged that Seán would live with the Joyce family for a while until he got himself together and was able to look for work. He was anxious not to be a burden on anyone, but he needed home comforts for a time following the harrowing sea journey. Honor was happy to mother him, and as the days passed, the colour came back into his face. With good food he gradually filled out and he could feel his strength came back bit by bit.

The neighbours were all on the lookout for work for him, and the billboards were scrutinised on a daily basis. There were many positions for labourers, for miners to travel to other states, for supervisors in factories, but none for school teachers. 'Not as of yet,' Honor would say optimistically, 'but in time there will be something.'

Mary-Anne, in the meantime, carried on with her work for the Wiseman family. She told Miss Janine of the arrival in New York of her former school teacher, for her young charge had always been interested in the details of Mary-Anne's life before and since she had come to America. Many a long afternoon had been spent by the two girls in this way, talking about Ireland and the goings-on over there.

'Some day, Mary-Anne, I will cross the sea to Ireland,' Miss Janine remarked one day. 'You have told me so much about Moneen and Galway that I would know my way around the highways and byways blindfolded.'

'Maybe you will, Miss,' Mary-Anne agreed, 'and by that time the Famine will have passed away and Ireland will healthy again. You will visit me in Moneen and I will show you the fields and rivers, the trees I climbed, the rocks high above the village. You'll see Ireland and you will love it as I do.'

* * *

87

THREE weeks after Seán Thornton arrived in New York, he was summoned to the home of Dr and Mrs Wiseman. They informed him that they were anxious that their daughter's education was being neglected, due to her delicacy, and would Mr Thornton consider taking some lessons with her for a couple of hours each day? The fact that Seán had some proficiency in the French language was greeted with delight, as they remarked of the great advantage it was for a young lady to have a European language, and that they were planning that Miss Janine would in time travel to Europe to broaden her outlook. When Seán eagerly accepted the proposal, her parents were very pleased at the way things had worked out to everyone's advantage.

Seán couldn't believe his good fortune in securing a position so soon. That evening in the apartment, there was a small celebration. Mary-Anne was there on her 'hours off', and Bina and Arthur also arrived to add their congratulations. It was Mary-Anne's first visit home since Seán had arrived and she felt quite shy in his presence.

'So, Mary-Anne, you and I will be working under the same roof!' Seán remarked with delight as they cleared away the ware. 'Are you happy there?'

'Oh, yes, I am very happy and content,' Mary-Anne answered. 'I do my work well so there is no quibble. You will find the same if you do what has to be done and do it to the best of your ability. Miss Janine is a very good and quiet girl; you will get on well with her. She is due back from her grandmother's home tomorrow.'

'Yes,' Seán said, 'I will have my first opportunity to meet my new pupil then.' He lit his pipe and looked at Mary-Anne carefully before asking, 'Tell me, Mary-Anne, have you settled any better than before? Are you still anxious to go back to Ireland?'

Mary-Anne's eyes filled with tears. She so hoped that Seán would understand her longing for home; if he didn't, she knew she would feel so unhappy. Mam and Dad were impatient with her at times about this wish to return across the ocean, and for a long time she had felt that Seán was the only one who understood her yearning for home.

'Have a bit of sense, child,' her father often said when she spoke of going home. 'There is not a thing for any of us over there.'

'You should be happy to have a roof over your head, plenty to eat and a little money to spend.' Her mother's voice would have a stern note in it. 'Can't you be happy with us all together and no trouble on us?'

Mary-Anne turned to look at Seán, at his steady blue eyes and kind face, and said, 'It is the dearest wish of my life to go back home again, to see our little village, to walk the fields and hills. I don't want to die in this land, good and all as it is to us... I want to be buried with my kin in Moneen. Nothing else will do for me.' She could feel the tears trickling down her face as she spoke and, embarrassed, made haste to wipe them away.

Seán Thornton looked at her. His heart knew that this girl was special to him. He placed his hands on her shoulders, looked into her misty eyes and said, 'Mary-Anne, you can depend on it, you will go back home to Ireland. I will see to it that your wish comes true.' He flicked away a tear and, bending down, kissed her wet cheek gently.

It seemed the most natural thing in the world to Mary-Anne that she should rest her head on his shoulder.

THAT night Mary-Anne had a dream. She dreamt that she was back again in Moneen. It was a sunny day, the road was dry and dusty, and she was on her way to school. Running ahead of her were Katie Mongan, Mairtín Connor, Bairbre Lidon and Seán Óg McDonagh. She called to them to wait for her, and they turned around and waited for her to catch up with them. When she tried to run her legs just wouldn't work for her; she had to struggle to take one step and then another. She tried to get her legs to move faster by gripping each leg with her hands and lifting then one after the other. Bairbre called, '*Déan deifir*, Maire-Áine, *déan deifir.*' But Mary-Anne could not move. Tears ran down her face. '*Táim ag teacht... fan liom, fan liom,*' she cried. The four children backed away from her slowly. '*Fan liom, mais é do thoil é, fan liom,*' she begged. She could not see their faces clearly through the mist which surrounded them. The four began to recede into the distance, away, away, until she could not see them any more.

Mary-Anne awoke with the tears streaming down her face, her heart thundering, her breath coming in gasps, and crying aloud, '*Fan liom, fan liom...*'

*Wait for me. Wait for me...*

Still shaking, she lay awake in the darkness. The dream had brought all the sorrow and grief back to her. She knew that Katie, Mairtín and Bairbre had died in the Famine, and that Seán Óg McDonagh had moved away with his family to Canada. What was the reason for this dream? I'll pray for them, she thought. Maybe they want me to pray for them... Poor Katie, Mairtín and Bairbre. She missed them so much. 'The light of heaven to them,' Mary-Anne murmured aloud.

It was near dawn before she slept again.

TWO days later there was a note for Mary-Anne when she went to the kitchen to prepare breakfast for Miss Janine. It had been hand-delivered, and when she opened it she recognised her dad's handwriting.

'*Come to see us when you can. Do not worry, nothing is wrong. Your fond father, Jamesy Joyce.*'

Mary-Anne was amazed. She had never had a letter from her dad in all the time she had been working for the Wiseman family. It had to be about something very important; he would never otherwise have gone to the trouble of putting pen to paper, a task he did not enjoy. Mary-Anne had memories of him sitting for hours at the kitchen table as he tried to compose a letter about something or other. The top of the pen would be chewed to bits and the sweat would stand out on his forehead. His schooling had been of the hit-and-miss variety, and his handwriting was not good. His insistence that his only living child should benefit as much as possible from schooling had kept Mary-Anne at school long after many others had left. 'Education is no heavy load to carry, *alanna*,' he'd say. 'To be able to read and write is a godsend, so keep to your schooling. You'll be glad in years to come.'

Mary-Anne was due an hour off that afternoon, which she had planned to use to do her 'writings' for Master Thornton. This was a task she enjoyed, but now, however, she would walk to Coburg Street and find out why her parents had wanted to see her.

When she took Miss Janine her breakfast she found her charge somewhat agitated.

'Is there something bothering you, Miss?' asked Mary-Anne as she settled the tray on the bedtable.

'Oh, Mary-Anne, I am so excited. Your friend, Seán Thornton, will be giving me lessons today,' Miss Janine informed her. 'It will be such a change for me. My life has been dreary of late...'

Mary-Anne was relieved. 'I'm glad you will be occupied today, Miss,' she said. 'This afternoon I will be visiting my parents. I received a letter today requesting me to come.' She plumped up the pillows and settled her charge to eat. 'Now, do eat a good breakfast, and when you are finished I'll help you to get dressed and ready for your first day at school.'

Miss Janine giggled. 'It is comical, isn't it? Here I am, almost eighteen years old, and it's like going to school for the very first time.'

Miss Janine looked very pretty this morning. There was colour in her face and her eyes were shining. She looked a very different girl from the wan creature she had been when Mary-Anne first set eyes on her.

\* \* \*

IT SEEMED to Mary-Anne, anxious as she was to discover why she had been summoned home, an age before she was climbing the stairs of her parents' tenement in Coburg Street. Now at last she tramped up the stairs, amid the sounds of children crying and people talking, and the smell of cabbage cooking – all the familiar noises and aromas of their tenement home.

'Ah, there you are, *a grá*,' her mother greeted her with a hug. 'You're just in time for a bite to eat.'

'Mam, I had a message from Dad to come home. Do you know what is on his mind?'

'Your dad will tell you all about it when he comes in.' And despite Mary-Anne's entreaties, no more information would her mother give to her.

But she was not to be kept waiting long: her father walked through the door, and to Mary-Anne's great relief, he was smiling. Her heart leapt. 'Dad, I am home as you asked. Why did you want to see me?'

'Well, *a stóir*, sit down there. You and I have to have a little talk.' Her dad took out his pipe and began to ready it.

'A talk about what?' Mary-Anne could hardly bear the waiting. 'Oh, Dad, tell me quick.'

Now that his pipe was lit and going properly, Jamesy set himself comfortably in the rocking chair.

'I had a visit from a young man yesterday,' he said contentedly, 'a fine strapping lad by the name of Timothy O'Connor. He asked for my permission so that you and he could walk out together. Did you know about this, Miss?'

Mary-Anne could feel her face redden, and she felt she wanted to hide behind the door. 'Oh yes, I did know,' she said confusedly. 'At least he said he would call – you see, I met him, or he met me, one day...'

'Take it aisy, Mary-Anne,' her dad laughed. 'Tell me about this meeting – nice and slow now, mind you.'

So Mary-Anne told about meeting Tim outside the house, first in the heavy snowfall and then again on her trip to the store, and about how he had said he would call to seek permission from her parents to walk out with her. Her mam and dad listened intently.

'Now Mary-Anne,' her dad asked, 'would you yourself like to walk out with this young man?'

'I think I would.'

'Only if you're sure now, *alanna*?'

'Yes, yes, I'm sure,' Mary-Anne said shyly, but happily.

'Your mam and myself are in agreement on this. We feel that this young man is respectable and mannerly, and we are both in favour of you going walking out with him. Isn't that right, Mother?'

'Yes, I think he is a fine young man,' her mother agreed.

'Tell me, Dad, what happens now?' Mary-Anne asked. 'What do I do?'

'You do nothin', Miss. This Tim O'Connor will be callin' on me next week for my answer,' her dad said, 'and after that he will come to have a meal here with us on your next day off, and after that... we'll see. Now that that's settled, we'll eat.'

Mary-Anne smiled happily at both of her parents. She was looking forward to seeing Tim again.

ON her way back to Gramercy, Mary-Anne fell to wondering about Seán and his work with her charge, Miss Janine. It was a mercy that Dr Wiseman had been on the lookout for a tutor, and that Seán had been available. He would be independent now, and be able to live on his own, which he was anxious to do, so as not to be 'putting out' her parents.

Entering the house and going to Miss Janine's rooms, Mary-Anne found her in a fever of excitement.

'Oh, Mary-Anne – I have so much to tell you about my day!'

The two girls sat down before the fire, as the evenings were still a little cool, and chatted together about the day's happenings. Miss Janine was particularly taken with

Mary-Anne's 'romantic news', as she put it, and was eager to hear about Tim O'Connor and how she felt about 'walking out' with him.

'I have never had the opportunity to walk out with anyone,' she said sadly. 'Being unwell for so long means there are very few parties to which I would ever be invited. Here I am, almost eighteen, and I have never really had much opportunity to converse properly with young men.'

Mary-Anne, feeling content with her own life just then, sympathised with her and, on impulse, said, 'Would your mama have a party for you to celebrate your birthday, do you consider?'

Miss Janine clapped her hands. 'What a wonderful notion! I am getting better day by day, and it would be good for me to have a party. I will ask Mama and Papa this evening at dinner.'

The two girls spent a very pleasant couple of hours before dinner planning the party and the guests they would like to have at it.

'You may ask Tim O'Connor to my party, and I will ask my tutor, my new tutor,' Miss Janine laughed.

Mary-Anne was taken aback. She had not, in truth, considered that she would be a guest at the party. She was not the social equal of her young mistress, she knew, and said so.

'But Mary-Anne, you are my dearest friend and my companion, and I will be so much more healthy by then, Mama and Papa cannot refuse me,' Miss Janine said confidently.

THAT night Mary-Anne lay in her bed, too excited to sleep. She had never been to a proper party in her life. What would she wear? She would have to get something nice, and pretty slippers – her boots just wouldn't do for such an occasion. Would Tim come to the party if she invited him? Would Seán? They might both feel out of place in such a situation, she knew. But she hugged herself in anticipation and eventually fell asleep, happily planning her wardrobe for the big event.

# CHAPTER 13

A WEEK or so later, Mary-Anne was surprised to find another letter awaiting her.

*'Come home on Thursday in time for dinner. Your fond father, Jamesy Joyce.'*

She hastened to advise Mrs Wiseman that she would require an afternoon off on Thursday, and was pleasantly surprised when the lady mentioned that plans to celebrate Miss Janine's eighteenth birthday with a party were already under way.

'My poor little girl, her life has been very restricted. We expect that in giving this party for her we will be creating an opportunity for her to improve her social life.' Mrs Wiseman smiled pleasantly at Mary-Anne. 'You have been such a help to my daughter. She is very happy to have you as her companion. Thank you, Mary-Anne.'

Cheerfully and happily, Mary-Anne set off for Coburg Street, where she found Tim sitting in her parent's apartment, dressed in a high-collared coat and black trousers, his peaked cap tucked into the waistband, and his hair neatly brushed. He looked the most respectable of young men, although a trifle nervous. Mam and Dad were also dressed in their Sunday best, she was delighted to see, and Mam had prepared a very special meal in honour of the occasion.

Conversation was rather stilted at the outset, and Mary-Anne in particular was unusually shy, but gradually they relaxed and in the end there was a deal of laughing and merriment, as Tim's naturally happy personality conquered his obvious shyness. Before the evening was over it was clear to Mary-Anne that Mam and Dad were very keen on the young man. The evening flew so much so that they were surprised when, at seven, Tim – who had to report for evening duty – rose to make his apologies, thanked Mam and Dad for the lovely meal and politely asked Mary-Anne to accompany him to the door when he was leaving.

'What evening would suit you to come out with me, Miss Mary-Anne Joyce?' Tim asked as they descended the stairs.

Mary-Anne smiled at his way of giving her her full title. 'I will be free on Wednesday next from two o'clock,' she said.

'Good,' Tim said. 'I'll arrange my duties for that day. Will I call to Gramercy at two, then?'

Mary-Anne was overcome with shyness. After all, she thought, she had never walked out with a young man before.

'Now come along, Miss Joyce, have you an answer for me at all?' her persistent suitor pressed her.

'That'll be grand, Mr O'Connor – I mean, Tim,' she finally managed to say.

'Good,' he said. He looked delighted. 'I'll be seeing you outside your place then, Wednesday, say about fifteen minutes after the hour?' He shook her hand politely and went out on to Coburg Street, loosening his collar stud as he walked. As Mary-Anne was turning to walk back upstairs, he stopped, turned around and made an elaborate bow, sweeping the ground with his cap.

'Good evening to you, Miss,' he said grandly, and turned and swung along the street in fine fettle.

Mary-Anne was still giggling at his carry-on when she pushed open the door of the apartment.

'There's a grand fella for you,' her mam said. 'Not a bit afraid to talk and him with a good job in the police force too.'

Mary-Anne agreed happily, and proceeded to tell her mother all about the planned party for her charge. She was a little concerned about what she should wear and wanted to hear her mother's opinion on this very important matter.

'Your Aunt Bina and myself will come up with something suitable, don't you worry,' her mother said. 'You'll not feel out of it. You will look grand entirely, mark my words.'

Mary-Anne was content with that and set off for Gramercy with a happy heart. She was walking out with a handsome young man, and she was going to go to a big party. Life in New York suddenly seemed better.

AS Mary-Anne went about her duties in the house, she occasionally met Seán. One day he met her carrying the hot-water can up the stairs to her mistress's bedroom.

'Mary-Anne, let me take that for you,' he said.

'No, really, I'm used to it,' Mary-Anne protested, but in truth it was very heavy and she was relieved when he insisted on taking it from her and carrying it as far as the bedroom door.

'This can is much too heavy for you,' he said. 'Is there no young lad around the place to take it up for you?'

'I am used to it, 'tis no bother to me at all,' Mary-Anne laughed. 'When I came here first my arms used to be half dead, but now it's fine.'

'Whenever I am available I will carry the container up the stairs for you,' Seán insisted. 'You'll have a crith on your back in no time.'

'How are you liking teaching Miss Janine?' she asked him. 'She is a sweet girl.'

'She is that indeed. She has led a very quiet life because of her being delicate,' Seán said. 'I hear that her parents are planning a birthday ball for her. That should be a fine turnout.'

Mary-Anne smiled at him. She enjoyed meeting him about the house – not just for his help, but because she had noticed that whenever she was in Seán Thornton's presence she felt at peace with herself. The persistent ache which she had carried around inside her for the past three years had dulled somewhat since Seán's arrival. It was as though going home to Ireland did not seem as impossible as it once had – her return was just a matter of time, that was all. Seán was her comfort and her confidant. Even though they no longer had a need to write to each other, they had many conversations together whenever the opportunity arose, and Mary-Anne found herself looking forward to them more and more.

SEAN himself had not been idle in his free time since starting work. He had been learning a little of the lifestyle of many of the Irish people since their arrival in America. The work in which many of them were engaged was difficult, he discovered, and in many cases downright dangerous. He particularly resented the conditions in the sewing factories, where the women and children were crowded together in unheated, badly lit rooms. At times, in these buildings, the doors would be locked, rendering escape virtually impossible should a major catastrophe such as fire break out. He often remarked to Mary-Anne that people were complacent and inclined to take the view that the importance of having a job superseded any other consideration. Didn't she think that safety in the workplace was vital, and that comfortable working conditions were only mild expectations for anyone?

'Mary-Anne,' he queried one day when they were having their afternoon meal in the kitchen, 'have you ever been in any of those places?'

'No, never,' she answered. 'I have listened to Aunt Bina, though – she worked in one for a short time and was glad to get out of it. She said in the summertime the heat was dreadful, no air coming in, windows and doors barred. The women would swoon flat on to the floor and the other women would shout and roar to get the attention of the forewoman so the doors would be opened. Oftentimes the women would be left there on the floor until the bell sounded for closing time. Aunt Bina often told me of the pale complexion and bad eyesight of these sewing women, and she said that lung problems were common in these places.'

'There are injustices in every country,' Seán said, 'but there should be an outcry against them. The people who work in these sweatshops should band together and demand better work conditions.'

'For a "peace-loving man", as you call yourself, Seán,' Mary-Anne said, 'you get involved in a lot of contentious issues.'

He leaned over the table. 'Mary-Anne,' he said urgently, 'I do it because someone must. People have rights and those rights must be guarded. No person should have to suffer any degradation in this day and age.'

Mary-Anne looked at him in concern. She knew he was right, but who knew what trouble he might get into if he became too involved?

# CHAPTER 14

PLANS for the birthday celebrations proceeded apace at the Gramercy home. A seamstress was constantly in the workroom, and fittings for the ball gown for Miss Janine were a regular feature. Janine and Mary-Anne themselves were kept busy filling out invitations and addressing envelopes. Mary-Anne had been formally invited to the ball by her employer, who had graciously enquired whether she had an escort for the evening or if there was anyone she would like to take to the celebrations. Later, both girls discussed the very important issue of 'escorts'. There were many young men, close acquaintances of the Wiseman family, who would be most suitable to accompany Miss Janine. However, Miss Janine had someone else in mind and she blushingly revealed to Mary-Anne that she was indeed contemplating inviting Seán Thornton to be her escort at the party.

'You will, of course invite your friend Tim O'Connor to come as your partner, won't you, Mary-Anne?' she enquired as Mary-Anne brushed her hair before bedtime.

'I am not sure, yet,' was all the answer Mary-Anne would give. Mary-Anne was puzzled at her own reluctance about asking Tim to escort her to Miss Janine's party. She argued with herself that Seán Thornton did not belong to her; he was a free man, he could do whatever he wished, and if he was happy to escort her mistress to her birthday celebrations, well, that was his decision.

Mary-Anne wanted to speak to her mam about this. Mam would know what was bothering her. She would go to Coburg Street as soon as she could, she decided. Mary-Anne smiled at Miss Janine and assured her that she would ask Tim, if the opportunity arose, to squire her to the ball. This satisfied the young lady and they resumed their pleasant task of arranging the invitation lists.

VISITING her home a few days later, Mary-Anne found her mam and Bina surrounded by swatches of voile, satin, taffeta in such lovely colours – pale green, cream, brown, yellow, amber – spread out so she could make her selection for her ballgown.

It was so difficult to decide! Each swatch had its own charm. Encouraged by the two ladies, Mary-Anne eventually decided on taffeta, in a lovely soft green. The material was held up against her, and it was agreed all round that the colour suited her perfectly. Mary-Anne thought it beautiful, she had never worn anything like it in her life. It would be a fairytale dress!

Later, when Bina had left, Mary-Anne told her mam that Miss Janine was planning to ask Seán to be her escort at the ball.

'You seem to mind about that,' Mam said.

'Yes, I do mind. Am I being very selfish, Mam?' asked Mary-Anne.

'Maybe a wee bit possessive, lovey. After all, you have a beau of your very own now, and anyway Master Seán isn't going to marry the girl, is he?'

Mary-Anne had to laugh, and agree that her mam was right, as usual. But still she felt uneasy.


WEDNESDAY morning found Mary-Anne in a high state of nerves. She dropped the soap on the floor as she was washing Miss Janine, tried to retrieve it and almost ended up in the hip bath along with the young lady.

'My, my, Mary-Anne, you are in a tizzy today,' Miss Janine chided her gently. 'Is it because you are walking out with Tim O'Connor in the afternoon?'

'Oh, I am sorry, Miss.' Mary-Anne finished wiping the suds. 'I am a wee bit anxious. What on earth will I converse with him about?'

'Silly Mary-Anne' was all the consolation her mistress offered, not being any better versed in the subject of young men than her companion.

MARY-ANNE spent a good deal of time deciding what she would put on for her first outing with Tim. Miss Janine had, on occasion, given her coats, dresses, under-things and shoes which she considered were no longer fashionable. Mary-Anne had received these with grateful thanks and delight, and she had fitted a curtain around a small alcove in her room, behind which she hung her precious clothing. Her bonnets were set out on a shelf above the 'wardrobe', and these she carefully covered with tissue paper to protect them from dust.

After a lot of fitting on and trying out the various garments, she eventually decided to wear the brown riding-coat-style dress which was buttoned from just above the waist down to the hem. Underneath this she wore a pretty yellow habit shirt with a turndown collar. The skirt was gathered at the waist and reached to the ground. She wore her prettiest bonnet, decorated with ribbons which matched her shirt, and which she tied in a bow under her chin. Her little high-buttoned boots just peeped from beneath her gown, and she carried her small reticule.

Miss Janine clapped her hands in pleasure at the lovely picture Mary-Anne presented.

'You look so pretty, Mary-Anne,' she exclaimed. 'Tell me, do, if you are still in a dither about meeting your friend Tim?'

'I am a little,' Mary-Anne confessed. 'It is my very first time walking out with anybody.'

'Never you mind,' her mistress encouraged her. 'You will have a wonderful time. Now promise me that you will tell me all about your evening when you return to the house.'

Mary-Anne promised faithfully that she would, and, bidding goodbye, went downstairs to the lower hall.

At a quarter past two precisely she observed the highly polished boots of Mr O'Connor pause above the steps and then begin to descend. When the door knocker sounded, she opened the door to confront a very finely turned-out young man. Tim wore a double-breasted coat, close-fitting to the waist, reaching to above the knee, and buttoned down the front. It had underrevers, and beneath these he wore a waistcoat, a high-collared shirt and a cravat. His hair was carefully combed and styled. He looked so splendid that it took Mary-Anne several seconds to recognise this fashionable young man as Tim, the police officer.

Tim, for his part, had never seen Mary-Anne looking so beautiful. He bade her the time of day, and politely assisted her up the steps and on to the pavement. They proceeded to walk along the avenue – a good deal of space between them, it must he said, and also a silence which neither of them could break until Mary-Anne tripped on a loose stone and Tim quickly prevented her from having a nasty fall.

'Have you been at the poteen before you came out?' he wanted to know.

Mary-Anne could only laugh at his impudence, and they got on famously after that. Mary-Anne mentioned the birthday ball, and shyly asked Tim if he would care to accompany her to it. He readily agreed and took the opportunity to tuck her hand through his arm, pointing out that she might trip over again ...

Most of the passers-by greeted Tim as they passed them on the way to the park. It made Mary-Anne proud to think that he was so popular.

'Everyone seems to know you, Tim,' she said.

'Oh, sure I'm as well known as a beggin' ass,' he laughed. 'I've been around this beat goin' on for three years now, you know. It's a great help in my work to know the people of the area. Then, if anyone has a problem, they can always come to me, or I could go to them.'

Mary-Anne was interested in Tim's work, and plied him with questions until they reached the park.

'Now,' he said in a gentlemanly fashion, 'shall we sit here a while and enjoy the lovely day?'

'That would be very nice,' said Mary-Anne demurely. They sat watching the birds, looking at the flowers and talking about this and that until Tim said,

'Are you hungry, Mary-Anne? I know a grand place where we'd get something to eat, just above Wyndham Street.'

'Yes, I am a little,' she answered. 'That would be nice.'

Tucking her arm into his again, Tim led her across the intersection, past the little church where Mary-Anne attended for Sunday Mass, and across to the little tea-rooms just beyond it.

They were heartily welcomed by the proprietor, evidently yet another friend of Tim's.

'Mary-Anne,' he said, 'this is Frau Lise Grüber, the greatest cook ever to come out of Germany. She makes the best apple strudel in the world. Frau Lise, meet Mary-Anne Joyce from Ireland.'

Mary-Anne shook hands with the plump, fair-haired woman, whose braids were worn coronet-fashion, and whose red and white gingham apron matched the table covers in the gleaming tea-rooms.

'You like America, Fraulein?' Frau Grüber smiled. 'It is a great country, do you agree?'

'It is indeed,' Mary-Anne agreed. And at that moment she didn't miss Ireland at all.

'For what you wish?' asked Frau Grüber, settling them at a table by the wall. 'We have spiced beef, veal, stew, dumplings and apple strudel...?'

'Apple strudel will be just fine,' Mary-Anne said, overwhelmed by the choice, 'and lemonade please.'

'I will have the same,' Tim decided.

As they ate, Mary-Anne realised that she was enjoying herself. The strudel was delicious, and she no longer felt awkward sitting opposite Tim. She did not spill her drink or drop any of the cutlery, as she had feared – indeed, the thought of such a possibility had kept her awake far into the previous night ...

She was quite disappointed when it was time to leave and return to Gramercy Avenue. Having agreed to meet again on the same day next week, they shook hands solemnly on the steps of the house, and bade each other goodbye.

Mary-Anne chanced to look around before she went down the steps and discovered Tim looking back as well. She gave him a little wave, and he, with a wide grin, gave her a slick salute before continuing smartly on his way.

WHEN Mary-Anne arrived upstairs, her mistress was in a fever of anticipation as to how she had got on, and she settled herself comfortably on the *chaise-longue* for a long discussion. She was hungry for every detail – how handsome Tim had looked, what they had talked about, where they had walked, what they had eaten – and they were quite unaware of how time was passing until the clock chimed, reminding them of the late hour.

Mary-Anne went happily to bed and slept soundly, with no worries to disturb her as on the previous night.

# CHAPTER 15

THE house was in a fever of excitement as the day for the ball drew near. The servants polished and shone the floors and furniture, took the carpets out to the gardens and beat them to remove dust and grime, and took the curtains down and hung them out in the air to freshen them for the big event. Cook demanded extra assistance in the preparation and cooking of the vast amount of food, and there was much dashing up and down stairs with supplies from the local stores.

Herr Weinrich, Miss Janine's dancing teacher, was requested to give her special tuition in the steps of that most graceful of modern dances – the waltz.

A heavy-set man, sporting side whiskers, he was surprisingly light and nimble on his feet. Miss Janine insisted that Mary-Anne learn the steps also, and they both thoroughly enjoyed their daily dance lessons. They practised together, taking turns to 'lead', and imitating Herr Weinrich's heavy Austrian accent, counting '*Von – too tree, von – too tree*' as they swooped and glided around the room before collapsing in giggles on the day-bed.

Miss Janine's ballgown was finished and hanging under dust covers in her wardrobe. She spent many hours arranging and rearranging her hair, trying out creams on her face, soaking her hands in lemon juice and lanolin, and putting cucumber wedges on her eyes to help them to shine and glow. Mary-Anne had little time to herself, what with all the to-ing and fro-ing going on in the house, and seemed to spend a great deal of time brushing and combing her mistress's hair, wrapping it in rags to encourage ringlets, and supervising the selection of necklaces and earbobs which might or might not suit the big evening ahead.

Mary-Anne's own dress was ready and she had been home for a fitting. Her mam and Bina were extremely proud of their handiwork and of how well it looked on Mary-Anne. In pale green taffeta, it had a long-waisted bodice draped with folds to form a V-shape to the waist which was encircled with a wide sash in a contrasting shade. The neckline was half-high and had a ruching trim. The long sleeves were full and caught in at the wrist with a neat band. The full skirt reached to the ground and had two flounces edged with lace. Her little evening slippers were covered in the same material as her dress, and Bina had given her a gift of a lovely delicate fan which had belonged to her own mother.

'M'anam, is cailín dathúil gléigeal thú, a stóir,' her dad exclaimed when he arrived to view the new dress, and indeed Mary-Anne did feel beautiful.

'Young Mr Tim will be the proud lad when he shows you off at the ball,' Mam said. 'Won't it be grand to be there to see all the lovely clothes? It 'll be a great occasion altogether.'

'Yes, 'tis a far cry from the sadness and despair which we knew at home in Ireland,' her dad agreed. 'This country is good to us, no doubt about it.'

Yes, Mary-Anne thought to herself, it has been good to us. She had walked out with Tim once more, and they had visited many places of interest in the city, avoiding the shanty areas on the outskirts. Again they had come to Frau Grüber's tea-rooms for more apple strudel. This time they ate it covered in cream and sprinkled with cinnamon.

They were in no way awkward with each other and the afternoon was spent discussing the way in which they saw their lives going in the future. Tim was studying law and criminology at night school, and he planned to work to help all the people who were unjustly treated, and who had no one to help them redress the wrongs put on them.

'Mary-Anne, you wouldn't believe the terrible things people do to each other,' he told her. 'The poor emigrants are led astray by the fly boys who do meet them off the boats, and then they are duped into parting with the little bit of money they might have on them.' Tim's naturally friendly face became stern and firm as he spoke.

'We thought we'd be well away from that kind of thing when we came to America,' Mary-Anne agreed. 'But I suppose there are bad folk everywhere, and they latch on to the poor creatures who have no one to look out for them when they step off the boats here.'

'In time to come I will do what I can to help them,' Tim promised, and they walked companionably home, debating the ways of the world.

NOW, on the evening of the ball, the air was filled with excitement. The carriages and barouches were letting off their passengers, and there was much hustle and bustle as the ladies in their magnificent gowns and supported by the arms of their escorts ascended the steps to the great hall. The clip-clop of the horses' hooves and the jingling of their harness echoed around the avenue, and the shouts of their drivers and the calling of the grooms added to the sound. A great feeling of excitement pervaded the street.

Inside the house, the main hall had been set out for the evening's dancing. The large room was gaily decorated with bunting and garlands of flowers. On each step of the stairs were large decorative pots filled with geraniums, hydrangeas and oleanders. The chandeliers and candelabra flickered and glowed with a myriad candles, and on the first landing the small group of musicians were tuning their instruments. Supper was to be served in the dining-room, which was equally magnificently decorated.

Miss Janine and her parents stood in the receiving line inside the inner doors. Miss Janine's gown, in soft misty blue silk, had a close-fitting bodice that set off her shoulders and draped across the front with a V-shaped décolletage filled in with a chemise of lace. The sleeves were bouffant with a lace-trimmed flounce at the wrist.

The wide-based skirt, falling full to the floor, had five flounces trimmed with matching lace. Her blue silk evening slippers showed just below the hem of the dress, and she wore white evening gloves and carried a lace fan. Her hair, unadorned but for a white rose, fell in ringlets from a centre parting to her shoulders, and her earbobs flashed and shimmered in the lights.

Miss Janine's cheeks, once so pale and wan, were glowing, and her eyes sparkled with all the excitement of the evening. She looked beautiful, and many a young man observed her with startled wonder, apparently not having ever noticed this rather special young lady before.

At a given signal, the musicians struck up a slow waltz and Dr Wiseman led his daughter on to the floor for the first dance of the evening. Seán Thornton, dressed in a black broadcloth suit with a white ruffled shirt and silver tie, led Mrs Wiseman out to join the dancers, and when they had completed one circuit of the dance floor, the general body of guests joined in. The swirling gowns of the ladies, as colourful as a summer garden, and the frock coats, tight-fitting breeches and silk stockings of the young men combined to give a delightful appearance to the occasion.

Mary-Anne stood with Tim O'Connor, rather splendid in his dress uniform, and watched the proceedings from just beside the band. She looked 'as sweet as a flower', as Tim had told her when he called to accompany her upstairs to the 'ballroom'. Since Tim was not very expert at waltzing, he had suggested that they should not join the crowd on the floor just yet. The polka was more in his line, he informed her, and when it was called at the next encore, he swept Mary-Anne out on to the floor with great dash and vigour.

Seán Thornton, standing behind the chair on which Miss Janine was resting following the dancing, noticed the two of them as they danced happily and energetically together. Again he realised with a start that this was not the starving child who had left Ireland, but a beautiful and intelligent young lady. For an instant he wished that he were her escort rather than Miss Janine's. In truth he felt rather awkward in his role, but since he was employed as tutor he could not possibly have turned down the invitation from his pupil. He was determined that he would have at least one dance with Mary-Anne, and decided to put his name on her dance card at the first opportunity.

Mary-Anne herself caught a glimpse of Seán as she was twirled around the floor, and thought to herself how well and handsome he looked in evening wear. She intended to keep a space or two on her card for his name. She had never danced with him, apart from sets, and very much wished to have a waltz with him should the opportunity arise during the evening.

When the supper bell sounded for the first round, Mary-Anne and Tim turned with relief towards the dining room, which was much less crowded and pleasantly cool. The tables were set out in rows, covered with white linen cloths and laden with an awesome array of food. The glitter of crystal, the shine of silver and the gleam of china added to the effect of the dishes of cold meats, vegetables, tureens of soups, fish of various kinds, salads, pastries, cakes, pies, selection of biscuits, sweetmeats, fruits, wines, lemonades, apple juices, cheeses of all sorts ... It was truly a magnificent spread, and the attendants effortlessly made sure that no one wanted for anything. Filling their plates with food and carrying cool drinks, Tim and Mary-Anne made their way to chairs set out along the walls.

After he and Miss Janine had been served, Seán espied Mary-Anne and her companion, and they made their way across the room to join them. Mary-Anne made the introductions, and Seán and Tim shook hands. Miss Janine smiled and greeted Tim shyly. They conversed on the turnout at the ball, the food, the music – it was small talk but it helped the initial shyness of both Tim and Miss

Janine to wear off. Tim was very gallant towards the young lady, wishing her a happy birthday and thanking her for including him on the invitation list. Seán took the opportunity to ask Mary-Anne for her card, and pencilled in his name alongside a slow waltz and a two-step. Tim, in the meantime, bowed to Miss Janine and requested that he should have the pleasure of a dance with her. She handed him her dance card and indicated that there was just one space left – for a waltz ...

When Seán and Miss Janine had gone to replenish their plates, Tim turned an anguished face to Mary-Anne. 'What am I going to do, Mary-Anne?' he implored. 'I cannot dance the waltz properly.'

Mary-Anne cast about for an idea. 'Tim, we will slip downstairs to the lower hallway and you can practise the steps there. I'll make sure you will do very well when it is time to take Miss Janine out for the waltz.' She had to giggle at the tortured expression on Tim's face. He was really in a fix, she thought.

'All right, we'll chance it,' he whispered.

The two of them left the dining room quietly, excusing themselves to Seán and Miss Janine. They tiptoed downstairs and found the place deserted. The servants had found vantage points for themselves on the upper stairway to watch the dancing and festivities down below.

'Now, Tim, place your arm here and take my hand like this,' Mary-Anne demonstrated.

Tim took Mary-Anne carefully in his arms, and they counted together: *one, two three – one, two three – turn, two three – again, two three...*

Gradually Tim got the rhythm and lost his nervousness. They swung up and down the hall, *one, two three – one, two three ...* His confidence regained, Tim willingly declared that he was now ready to return to the ballroom and dance the waltz with Miss Janine, and why he ever thought that the waltz was difficult he just could not understand..

When they returned to the ballroom the last encore of a set of polkas had just finished. Checking on her dance card, Mary-Anne realised that the next dance had Seán Thornton's name pencilled in against it. She looked around for him, wondering if he had forgotten, and she saw him making his way towards them. She could see him looking around for her, and when he caught sight of her a brief smile crossed his face. For an instant Mary-Anne felt as if there were only the two of them in that crowded room. She could see the blueness of his eyes, and she felt a warmth of happiness when he reached her side and said, 'May I have the pleasure of this dance with you, Mary-Anne?'

The band were again playing a slow waltz, and Seán led Mary-Anne into the mass of swirling dancers. He took her into his arms and they glided away. Seán was an excellent dancer and Mary-Anne felt that she was as light as a feather as they dipped and twirled to the beautiful Viennese music. They spoke not a word until the music stopped.

Seán did not release her at once. He looked down at her, smiled and said, 'Thank you, Mary-Anne mavourneen.'

They stood looking silently at each other for a moment, and then Seán led Mary-Anne back to where Tim was standing. The three of them stood together and watched Miss Janine as she and her partner spun around the floor in a fast-moving quadrille. Tim offered to get some cool drinks for the three of them. The time for the waltz was drawing near, and he had begun to have doubts again about his dancing ability. Some lemonade, he felt, would calm him.

Seán and Mary-Anne stood side by side watching the partygoers as they chatted and laughed during the interval. She was happy and content just to be with him, and when he asked her if she was enjoying the ball, she nodded and smiled up at him.

As if it were the most natural thing in the world, he took her hand and held it closely and warmly in his.

The musicians resumed their seats and the strains of the next waltz encouraged the dancers to take to the floor again. Looking somewhat nervous, Tim led Miss Janine on to the dance floor. She looked slight and delicate beside him, but did not appear in the least put out when he stumbled once or twice as the waltz began. Mary-Anne could see his lips form the words *one, two three – one, two three* as they circled around, but gradually the anxious look on his face was replaced by confidence as he settled into the rhythm. Once or twice he even attempted an over-elaborate twirl, which Miss Janine followed without a falter.

Mary-Anne watched them dancing together – the tall young man, proud in his uniform, and the fair-haired graceful girl. She looked at Seán, her dear schoolmaster and friend, and felt a warmth and peace steal through her. She hoped that life would always be this good for the four of them ...

THAT night Mary-Anne had a dream.

She was home again in Galway, and standing on the hills above the village. The smoke was rising from the chimneys, and there were people and animals moving around below through the fields. Her little terrier, Cú, was busy checking out the rabbit burrows, and in the distance the purple mountains shimmered in the sun. There was a man climbing towards her, a tall man. 'Mary-Anne,' he called and held out his arms to her.

She began to walk towards him and then to run, faster and faster, until she reached the haven of his arms and she heard him say, 'Mavourneen, mavourneen *dilís*.'

**Attic Press** hopes you enjoy *Mary-Anne's Famine*. To help us improve the series for you, please answer the following questions.

1. Why did you decide to buy this book?

_____

_____

_____

2. Did you enjoy this book? Why?

_____

_____

_____

3. Where did you buy it?

_____

_____

_____

4. What do you think of the cover?

_____

_____

_____

4. Have you ever read any other books in the BRIGHT SPARKS series? Which one/s?

_____

_____

_____

If there is not enough space for your answers on this coupon please continue on a sheet of paper and attach it to the coupon.

Post this coupon to **Attic Press**, 29 Upper Mount Street, Dublin 2 and we'll send you a **BRIGHT SPARKS** bookmark.

Name _____

Address _____

_____

You can order your books by post, fax and phone direct from:
**Attic Press**, 29 Upper Mount St, Dublin 2, Ireland.
Tel: (01) 661 6128 Fax: (01) 661 6176